THE VOICE OF
Silence

An Unmissing Link Flowing Eternal

TOM SADNAUR

authorHOUSE®

AuthorHouse™
1663 Liberty Drive
Bloomington, IN 47403
www.authorhouse.com
Phone: 1 (800) 839-8640

Published by AuthorHouse   09/26/2016

ISBN: 978-1-5246-3924-2 (sc)
ISBN: 978-1-5246-3923-5 (e)

Print information available on the last page.

Any people depicted in stock imagery provided by Thinkstock are models,
and such images are being used for illustrative purposes only.
Certain stock imagery © Thinkstock.

This book is printed on acid-free paper.

Because of the dynamic nature of the Internet, any web addresses or links contained in
this book may have changed since publication and may no longer be valid. The views
expressed in this work are solely those of the author and do not necessarily reflect the
views of the publisher, and the publisher hereby disclaims any responsibility for them.

ABOUT THE AUTHOR

With the Plan of releasing this work under a pen name because it was written prior to my current style that has been evolving, I decided to once again just go under Tom Sadnaur.

Tom Sadnaur is a hit or miss smash in your face futurist. I am an ever determined poet attempting to express a word to be worth a thousand pictures.

Seeing it or not, I know, down the road, I will be satisfied I gave my best shot to let my words live-on on paper. I don't care of other's opinions of the words I write down, as these words express my ideas and thoughts as I see put to lay them out to the world. When I move on I shall have peace that I have put forth effort in an attempt to achieve the calling of my dreams.

I am going to continue my work until I am satisfied I have said what I have to say, and even at that point I do not believe the poetic voice shall escape me. I figure the publishing of a half dozen works, more or less, shall put out a characteristic example of my use of written language. The more I get rejected the stronger I shall try and the harder I shall work, until the fancy is replaced.

As my craft has been evolving itself I am continually having these ah ha moments of ways to improve my style and skill. Such as the other day I write a note to myself in a new notebook I call "future work." And I say well, when the three works Iam completing at this time are behind me and the new ideas are gnawing at my soul, Iam going to try to rewrite a poem, paragraph, chapter, ect.. I have just written a few weeks earlier off of memory. Trying to remember the exact words and capture the same concept of the poetic message screaming for release.

This writing concept came to me the other day cutting my grass in a race against darkness. I kept stopping and going into the garage to jot down the lines spinning through my thoughts. I was pushing along in a big square and when I got back closest to the garage was about the same cycle as the line I would think up passing alongside those things of nature inspiring me.

Anyway I am doing my work on one of my current projects for upcoming publication and those lines I scribbled down are fitting right in. Yet I don't quite remember them the same as I wrote them, and I can not find the gas pump receipt I penciled them on.

Those words were like my children. I was looking for hours everywhere. I remember, pretty sure, after completing my chores outdoors, putting them in with the work they fit into so perfectly. But they are lost. So I will rewrite the verse the best I can remember and when the original resurfaces I shall combine the two into a better more complete version. When the movements are closest the kindred will connect routinely to eventually become one.

I am a glass half full type of guy. I spent four hours looking for a two inch by five inch scrap of paper, but maybe this could be a useful technique I could try on a future work. Lose the work and go back to it. Write it twice and compare and combine the two in order to write better more concise fiction. If that scrap of thoughts were where I had thought, I may never of had this idea for this new type of editing I would like very much to try on myself in an upcoming work.

It is all part of the developing and honing of a craft. The hardest part is having the confidence to get started. Once began the path will evolve to complete itself in a sharing of justice expressed through my writer's voice. I enjoy evolving my writing skills and hope that you enjoy listening as I grow.

The sad things written are supposed to give you an awareness and appreciation for the daily things we should be thankful for. The happy things written should make you take notice of just how thin the fragile strands are that delicately hold this breathing existence of ours together.

Anyway this is my second publication. Enjoy it. Also, as I grow as an author, and pass through this short midlife phase of boredom, enjoy my other works published and upcoming by Tom Sadnaur.

*I*T IS ALWAYS A BIT un-Earthing, or questionably disturbing if you will, when you begin a new year and the previous year's cache phrase is an obscure weather phenomenon or the new word added to the dictionary is that of a disease or a plague, or a syndrome. Often an acronym, SIDS, HIV, AIDS, SARS, UV INDEX, PDS, El Nino, arctic blast, polar vortex, CME, tropical drift, MERS, etc.., over all though aren't these phrases and terminology going to be the real characters in our story, the description of our lives, the translation of our history, the meaning of our destiny. Our past and future rolled into what we are at this moment in time, being the circumstances defining our society and diagnosing the natural interpretation of the uniqueness of our species, One of the Earth with the Earth in (or maybe not in) harmonious coexistence.

If it was all so simple. We could just use and make up happy words to write our story together. With such expressions as FUN and gay, EZ and so-so, QTZ and hip–hop, O.K. & Bueno, Sunshine and nappy-time, we could then whisk away in an eternal dream sleeping with the future joined with the present infinitely forever blissful in holy matrimony.

No. Ours is a bit of an unholy matrimony. Scarring is a good word to describe us. That's what we do to things even if we don't mean to or are unaware of it.

Many of our New Year's characters are the technological terms and slogans of man's intellectual superiority (web, internet, GPS, cell phone, IP, etc..), dribbled down to the hordes like bread crumbs to an ant, giving us (and the average third grader) the feeling of power and genius through the manipulation of devices we are really only able to plug in. Yet we are exceptionally smart and athletic being so, so quick with the fingertips, nailing those buttons with the professional agility and accuracy of an all-star caliber ballplayer. The hand may be quicker than the eye but the eye is no match for the quickness and speed of the mind as human kind delves into the unlimited potential the psych possesses with the heart and soul of our DNA, together being the singularities that make you and I one.

DNA. There is a memorable old one. Often medical jargon as well as scientific concepts and breakthroughs bounce into our language as easily as the laser sight of a kinetic rail gun off of an ICBM en route to the ER of an abortion clinic for those with MS, ALS, or special needs either mentally impaired or physically challenged as well as unwed agnostic mothers, victims of abuse, and those simply wishing to use the facility as a form of birth control. But seriously, it is unavoidable to forget about the mechanical terminology which pops-up at the end of the year re-writing the dictionary yesterday's culture adopted into the vocabulary as powerful everyday hands on slang incorporated into the speech of the masses wanton of the possession of the iconic hard goods which they cannot live without and must obtain to be on equal with those slithering around themselves. The CD, SUV, microwave, and other such characters so dear to the heart, were once fridges, light bulbs and autos. PC's and LLV's making garage bands (nerds banding in their garages) rich with their inventive ingenuity nurturing our mentality to a peaceful anxious bliss similar to a child on Christmas Eve. No different than Coca-Cola and the drab Model, whatever the heck letter Ford, draws the cravings of desire to be. A thing one cannot get on without, till all must possess these marvelos machines as a necessity to make those who tyrannize the wealth even more so to the fact, yet put the voiceless flocks to a job feeding each other the trademarks of joy they must consume. But it is all in the good as progress provides limitless potential to better those who desire to better themselves from the small encaging certitudes and convictions that others force upon them to keep us down. Thus we become happy.

So we become happy with the absorption of a mindset into the vocabulary we take for granted as if the slang of the day was always there in the double helix and not new but eternal, as if using a new word that describes a real thing we've known for two months creates and leaves a memory of there not ever being a time when the ideology, such as the internet, wasn't there, or say for example the telephone is a device as old as the dark ages. It all just becomes so common so fast that it is only new till you hear it once and then it becomes ancient as if it's always been there patiently waiting in a cosmic well of knowledge, but just not yet uttered in our Milky Way galaxy. The acceptance of society to excessively and unassumingly swallow these jolting monsters that propel us forward (as well as feed each owns satisfaction) in such a way saying that it is great for everyone to consume and possess infinity and extra in a jif or a spree, no make that at light speed instantaneous with sparkle and glowing bright, blinded (by our I-ism) to what the long term effects might be to society, evolution, the planet or even one's own immediate self and well-being.

There was a time (before the belief in filters and the increase of protection they extend) when practically every fashionable individual smoked one popular brand of cigarettes or another. Like a sugar the simple addiction didn't take much persuasion to penetrate and corrupt the swelling invincibility of youth. The advertisements portraying the sexy vitality of the oral fixation generated and expanded capital wealth in a style on par with the virility of the world's largest corporations. With the erection of its stylish status and symbolism the familiar packages enlarge the appeal to attain iconic household recognition like an obelisk in center square. A part of the GNP not much different than alcohol, coffee, or gasoline, the musty dank butt of the tobacco craze ignites and fuels economic growth till the greed snubs out the monetary resources it has bred. As its' dark secrets come to light a new type of economic growth emerges; in the court room, class-action.

Where does a person's money go to anyway? To what pleases the senses is the answer. The pennies people throw to a stick of gum or swig of soda add up to enormous sums eventually allowing one company to buy out another and the bigger buying out the smaller till pretty soon the tobacco plantation owns the factory producing oxygen tanks and the brewery partnership has an affiliation supplying Breathalyzers. Fast food chains open up health clubs next to their burger joints and all the while the premium joints are being sold in the coffee shops. So when it gets to the point where only a few enormous corporations own the market of the majority of business where is capitalism beyond a government controlled society where the wealth is put back into the nation instead of into the pockets of the wealthy few?

What are we for chewing the gum? Drinking the soda or the beer. Smoking the cigarette, eating the candy bar. For any of the indulgences of the senses? The vinyl albums and 8-tracks, CD's and MP3's. The phones and devices. Of course there are Surgeon General Warnings, censorship funds, AA, EPA, FDA, eating disorder groups, as well as restrictive laws, but what are we, the consumer? The commercials, billboards, and magazines tell us to go into the fantasy world and eternally consume the goods robotically on a beach overlooking a pleasant fiery sunset against a peaceful deep reddish-blue sky as a translucent yellowish full moon begins to rise above the hypnotic pulse of foaming ocean waves rhythmically amplifying its message to you. People are being told to feed their desires. It's acceptable to spend on the vices. It's encouraged. Without thinking about it ignore those next to you and do what feels good. Do what makes you feel like you are in a Super Bowl commercial. Alone behind closed doors go dial up some porn. Gluttonously feed the economy. So what are we, guinea pigs? Drones? No, just consumers. Consumers and contributors. Whether it be first hand, second hand, or even third hand, we are consuming the fruits of the Earth, nourishing the economy, sacrificing all shame, humility, and health only for each of us to play a part, albeit a small part, in contributing to mankind's mark on this planet as a person's inner religion has become a partnership of what is right, legally right, and that which pleases, hence allowing the miracle of forgiveness to rescue the exiled soul from eternal damnation.

So why shouldn't it be that the richest countries in the world also have the most health issues related to over consumption and self-inflicted disorders? Even with all the warnings and labels on our side trying to keep us safe, ultimately it is the ever expanding universe of the medical industry that will profit (and employ) the most by taking care of the sick and cancerous as well as the broken and disabled, including the self-inflicted disabled, who as witnesses dutifully answer the subliminal call of corporate advertisement with their vulnerable weakness of self-gratification which is a substitute for what is lacking in the fulfillment of their lives. So go ahead and get sick. It is good to get sick. If you have good insurance (if there is such a thing) some doctors can keep you believing you are even sicker, and ill and ailing even longer. While under the care of health professionals you will be helping to support the economy, as well as the many women and men (and their families) working in any one of the numerous facets of health related fields trickling down economic stimulation surpassed only by those working on some type of government payroll. It all depends on where you fit into the orderliness of the system.

Wilbur Notts was no exception to the frailties of the flesh as the feel good precursors of soda pop, ice-cream, and candy would temporarily quench his primordial childhood hankerings. Being an ordinary kid growing up in a time of national hardship these doses of gratification were looked at in a different way than one might think of in later eras and were much more appreciated and coveted as luxurious extravagances arousing moments of lavish fanciful escape. So when he returned home in early 1946 two packs a day wasn't uncommon for a GI to arbitrarily and irresponsibly burn up. After all in the army cigarettes were basically free so why not take a crack at them to lighten the tension. This was a natural continuation into adulthood. Adult candy so to speak. Later, after the war in 1953 when his son, Will Jr., was six, the vigorous youngster would *eat* his candy cigarettes so that he could emulate and be just like dad, and of course ice cream was always a common treat found in the Notts family icebox in times of plenty.

Luckily for Grandpa Notts (as Will Sr. was endearingly referred to for generations to come) the soda pop fizz wasn't too strongly evolved into a booze stimulation even though at the time a bit of boozing was acceptable treatment for "adjustment disorder". The true label PTSD wouldn't reach the tips of the tongues of mainstream vocabulary and awareness for another forty years, even as medical advancements were marching forward at a break neck briskness. Will Sr. was sharp and inherently sensible enough to not allow this transitory period of his early adult life to flow into full blown alcoholism, or interfere with the providing for his family and child. This family dedication could be what spurred his extended life on our Earth, and if not, definitely in the least, contributed to his many years of enhancing those existing around him.

After Pearl Harbor's sneak attack the seventeen year old Wilbur left home a boy willing to lie about his age if his mother would not have signed for him to enlist. Throughout his entire lifetime he never really talked much about what he saw and did. In this way the vibrant veteran was a quiet man after returning home with his grown-up habits and his war mementos as symbols of his duty and valor. Via an official war trophy system the GI was allowed, with the proper paperwork (wink, wink), to bring home one gun and one sword as personal souvenirs, but not being much of believer of guns in the home during times of peace the idealistic and practical Wilbur traded his complete Japanese type 99LMG paratroopers model (in carrying case) for a second ornate samurai sword which was in modern times more of a symbolic armament rather than a killing machine and thus to him more of a prized historical spoil than a contrivance to jostle back tucked away memories of bloodshed and death. So was his reasoning for unloading a device in which he had no desire of gripping onto and was going to dump off at the earliest convenience anyway.

In February 1946 Wilbur wasted no time proposing to his sweetheart the strawberry blond Irish Lass Margaret Mary. A Midwest boy he had met the Flushing native at a roller rink while on leave and wished to marry her the very same evening after talking with her all through the night on her front porch. Following many letters back and forth he finally reappeared on the last night of the window that he had promised to come back for her. Marge, haven given up, had gone to a movie thinking that she had been duped, but to her amazement and delight, as she returned from the Bijou walking down the sidewalk, the tall and handsome clean cut man in uniform was there waiting for her on the front steps. Unfortunately for him the marriage would have to wait until after Lent and would require permission for the twenty year old Margaret who wouldn't be of age until October. So after a June wedding they settled into their first flat back in his native Midwestern city. The newlywed's alone time however didn't last long as Will Jr. came along the following May.

It wasn't as if the entrance of little Will into their lives ended their story book relationship of everlasting immeasurable love, but rather on the contrary enhanced their life long and beyond universal bond. It would be safe to say that Will Jr. may have been doted on just a tiny bit, after all times were exceptionally good. Jobs were plentiful and the middle class was developing its own expanding niche in society. A few years after the arrival of Will Jr. the Notts's were pregnant once again, however complications during child delivery didn't allow the life-less twins to survive their passage into this world. After this traumatic failure of consciousness it was highly recommended by the doctors that Margaret have no more pregnancies because she most likely would not make it through the ordeal of giving birth to another baby. She was then obligated to exercise the use of the recommended birth control methods of the day and later in the early 1960's permitted to go on the pill. Ultimately the end result was that the young Will would grow up somewhat shielded as an only child.

Will Jr. was relatively easy to raise and was the favorite (albeit only) nephew of Will Sr.'s older brother, Henry Notts. Uncle Henry was like a second father, often watching little Will for the weekend so that Will Sr. and Marge could get away alone together for a short spell. Later when Will Jr. was a bit older the all American lad would come along with his parents on their camping trips as well as on other sporadic vacations with the family's shiny Air-stream trailer. Often Uncle Henry would also join the trio on an extended weekend camping excursion.

Even after the Notts family moved out to the suburbs beyond the bustle of the airport, Uncle Henry was still actively involved in many facets of little Will's upbringing, such as scouts and little league. Uncle Henry never married nor had any children. He was somewhat bitter and drank too much. Most of his pent up frustrations were due to the fact that he left an arm back on a beach in France. Even with the plethora of scientific, medical, and technological advancements propulsioning forward, in one of the few countries that wasn't war torn and rebuilding, doctors still weren't able to sew his arm back on, or give him a robotic one, or grow a new one for him in a lab somewhere using siphoned off secret German technology and experimentation. Those were the kinds of things people hoped for and saw in their imagination of the future. There was a trust in science, as well as in the government, to bring all the best to the people. Why would the government need to hide beneficial breakthroughs? And why would the government need to lie to the public when it is by the people and for the people? Eventually everybody knew and didn't care that it was going to be Van Braun's rockets that were going to send us to the moon (or to the stone ages depending on what was put on the tip of his "V3" rocket).

So why not a new arm for Uncle Henry? After all there was open heart surgery, artificial valves, and pace makers. Just don't be too liberal or you may cause a red scare and end up on a blacklist. And don't ever rock the boat, loose lips can sink ships. Ike and Dick they're for you; oh yeah sure they are. And Truman was that really a real name or some successful relative of Willy Loman from Death of a Salesman? Most of Uncle Henry's drunken ramblings, such as these, were dismissed as self-pity, anger, and irritation, but maybe it was that the scraps satisfying the majority of the sheep just didn't seem to be enough to Uncle Henry. Somehow he believed and just knew that there was more out there not being released, such things which could potentially better the lives of citizens like himself.

There was a brief period where availability of health care to all equally seemed to have a chance. A snowball chance in hell, maybe. President Truman proposed national health insurance and Ike also tried some, but the AMA lobbied strongly for the bills not to pass and raised fear of subpar socialized medicine. In Uncle Henry's regard, after the second World War government and military companies joined together to produce better prostheses and make the public more aware and accepting of the issues related to the loss of limbs and artificial replacements. In reality the improvements transferred to individuals like Uncle Henry at a glacier's progressive pace. Even with the National Academy of Science developing more functional and realistic appendages it wasn't until after the Vietnam War, some thirty or so years later, that electronic controls were introduced, and it would be over another fifty years or so after this before someone could simply design, scan, and produce their own one at home using their 3-D printer. Even so, in Uncle Henry's lifetime, by the time the electronic controls were coming out he was tired and suffering with frequent concentrated headaches which the Bayer aspirin in which he preferred could no longer offer relief to alleviate, and so he barely wore the cumbersome and uncomfortable hook that he had clamped onto for all those years. In his prime Uncle Henry had actually become stronger in his one arm than an average man might be in both of theirs. Another thing was the fact that he wasn't exactly rich and the latest and greatest, even after only being responsible for paying a co-pay, aren't exactly the cheapest, nor always even covered by health insurance.

Uncle Henry had a transhumeral prosthesis which is a replacement above the elbow, basically at the shoulder. With no elbow it is difficult for one to mimic the use of the arm. The hook on the end would open and close to grasp onto things in moderate fashion by shrugging the shoulder. If there was any type of a slightest plus to this situation for Uncle Henry it would have been for the strength and resilience of the materials used in fabrication, where the resourceful veteran might use the hook as a hammer or to go into red hot scalding water or to tear open a box or beer can that might normally rip open ones flesh. In a fist fight the nearly indestructible tentacle could fend off oncoming blows as well as deliver the final smash. To say these attributes were positives over having his own arm back would be untrue and were merely just novelties for the one armed man to display as a sideshow while tending bar at The Corner Tap.

Sometimes if things weren't going well for the Notts family Will Sr. could also get a little bitter, and eventually find himself at The Corner Tap to seek out Uncle Henry's curative cynosure, but this wasn't very often. One of Will Sr.'s favorite declarations of self-pity would be to wish that he never had left the army and the great life that existed there. With free food and housing to go along with nothing to do with all that money they were paying him; boy o boy, a twenty year or lifetime soldier would be set to retire rich and early, happily ever after. The matured young father would blabber that he'd reenlist right at that moment, and Uncle Henry would say, as he wildly swung his hook over his curly head, that he would go with to be a surgeon just as Wilbur simultaneously announced to Uncle Henry that he couldn't even make it as a cook in the Army. Then a bitter and disgruntled patron who was sick of listening to the fanciful demeanor would sarcastically yell out "why don't you bums go fight in Korea?" After a miniscule silence, which was extremely awkward and out of place for a drinking establishment, the subject would quickly change and the WurliTzer would somehow miraculously energize to life blasting out a patriotic anthem setting the tone for the next debate, leaving the last discussions forever forgotten.

Nobody expected the Korean War, or Police action (against communism) if you want to be technical. It was the Atomic bomb era. There was no longer a need for war. The big war had just ended. Wars shouldn't be happening until well down the road from this time. The United States was prepared to lead the advancing world into the next age. What is the government not telling us besides only telling us communism is evil? No we need to protect and interfere with every little nation that is experiencing civil disorder? Why can't the newly formed U.N. and NATO solve this diplomatically, with the use of the A-bomb deterrent and without sacrificing more of our innocent American boys? Holy Toledo were those trusting young men who joined the reserves completely caught off guard. The best advice of the day was to not wait for the draft, just enlist, get your hopefully uneventful year over with and return back to the safety of home and once again help contribute to the growth of the world's economic leading society. Many of those who enlisted got a letter from home saying that they had just been drafted, but since they volunteered first they would only need to willingly do the one year enlistment versus the two years required from being drafted.

Eventually, (with the help of conscription, ironically, to turn the tide of the unfolding predetermined events), the U.S. was able to get its military act and capabilities back together and somewhat updated from the surplus they went into the 1950's with, thwarting the communist Korean dictatorship back to the North. Forcing them to re-step their blitz back towards Russia, South Korea would remain free and democratic. There was a valuable lesson to be learned here. If the world was to go on with freedom and peace military expansion and development would be essential. Plowshares would have to be prepared to militarize at any time. Financing of a technological industrial military complex and its Ops, not unlike the recently defeated National Socialist Germany or the cold and ever threatening communist red army, would have to become an unrestrained expenditure necessary of future budgets true to the history and nature of man, not unlike the ancient Romans and other great empires who conquered before. Simultaneously much covert improvement would be needed over the techniques experimentally honed by the Oppenheimer clan in New Mexico.

Who ever said not to discuss politics, religion, or work in a bar hadn't spent much time in one because bellyaching and advice (mostly unsolicited) on two of those subjects recur in a perpetual cycle day after day and the third, religion, is ambiguous because most regulars religiously frequent the saloon which then becomes a chapel to them. Even on the rarer than rare occasion Will Jr. would accompany his father on a visit to Uncle Henry's work, the impressionable youngster was able to observe these discrepancies first hand while watching the progress of a card game (in between pinball) and overhearing the conversations of the many different personalities that formed the camaraderie of the establishment. The pre-pubescent hellion pretty much knew the name of every brand and type of liquor available at the time, as well as numerous swear words in a couple of different languages, in addition to some catchy card phrases and sarcastic come backs and retaliations such as for a small sampling: "two, four, you little whore," "No shit Sherlock," "shit the bed Fred," and something about laying in the weeds and being a weed layer, whatever all that meant. His developing imagination unboundingly wondered if this was some type of occupation or if one would actually lay dead weeds on the grave of someone who screwed them over as some type of disrespecting pay back or an afterlife curse. Even though Will Jr. was pretty much a coveted and spoiled "momma's" boy with the highest standards of moral upbringing his dad and uncle knew that a little exposure to the darker sides of reality would be beneficial for his journey into manhood, however Will Sr. didn't quite know the full extent of Uncle Henry's shadowy influence.

Spending a fair amount of time around his uncle, Will Jr. realized a person can learn something new about a loved one each and every day if time is spent communicating and actually listening. Uncle Henry speculated, with his negative objectivity and sarcastic demeanor, that history is a series of disinformation, sometimes deliberate, and sometimes not intentionally but just actually mistaken yet believed to be true. Our current understanding and awareness, he deduced, is derived from this disinformation and History, when it is figured out and set straight, is what organizes the knowledge and verifies the information and data, and it is only when civilization moves forward with hindsight and due investigation can the past be arranged into the correct order. Basically Uncle Henry was saying cover-ups can only last so long because eventually the ones who are hiding something have their time come to pass and as truths are dug up, or naturally trickled to the surface, the skeletons and secrets come out of the closets and history can then be accurately estimated and written without regard for protecting the now historic figures and entities which were concealing those bits and pieces of incriminating factual details long ago, even though the lengthier masked material evidence is kept buried and undisclosed the harder it is to believe as the forensic proof and facts become blurred pretty much leaving it up to the individual to decide to believe for their own self. Almost like the "lost" treasure hidden so well it is only discovered long long after the stashing and the concealers were never able to return and rejoin with the store to enjoy it anyway, making the act a selfish greed taken to the grave. So what is the point of it forever to remain only to be something that shall never again be appreciated and ultimately only be reclaimed by the Earth (if it was in fact of this Earth to begin with), and eventually the recycling powers of the universe. It just must be in the genome to hoard away prized personal possessions and memories containing dark secrets.

As with Uncle Henry and Will Jr. it is often through adversity and hardship that one is forced to advance their life and find their true way and purpose. Not always the probable foreseeable path through this life one might have previously anticipated and expected to find themselves on only a short time prior, a person fatefully becomes what they are and what they do. This was the case with Uncle Henry who found his calling (or it found him depending on how you look at it) and became very good at running (or rumming) a tavern. Always on top of sport's news, any and all the current events going down in the neighborhood, as well as anything else new and exciting (or glum) happening in the headlines, made the one armed man, (as he was frequently affectionately referred to by his regulars, for instance while bar hopping a group of fleeting best of friends might suggest "let's go have a drink with the one armed man," or "I wonder if the one armed man is tending bar tonight?"), all made him one of the best and well liked, almost famous, bartenders for miles around. Not even needing to earn a salary the upstairs lodging along with free food and drink made the tip money in his pocket a modest income, enough to make an average factory worker jealous and on par with his brother's romanticized military life. One of the colorful server's most familiar quotes was to ask a patron complaining about their job or money was "do you want to be rich or do you want to be famous?" But the catch was that the drunken whiner was never allowed to answer "both." Uncle Henry would give some bogus consolement about how you can be rich in other ways besides with money and one could be famous in their own right in their own circles. Uncle Henry would also argue that "if we really want to get rich we should start our own religion." Discussions would then jokingly wander between the religions of beer and sex until everyone agreed that a future religion worshipping technology would be the way to control the minds of the masses, as well as their pocketbooks, and hell they might as well make it a corporation.

Passing through the 1950's the young Will Jr. was able to experience and absorb the never ending head spinning changes that were happening throughout the decade on a regular basis. Color TV, FM transistor radio, many of the latest things proceeding on a fast pace to the future. It was the infancy stages of "modern" 20th century technology controlling the people and playing an extreme role in economic boom and bust. Each new breakthrough is like a log on the capitalistic conflagration causing it to blaze forth till it burns down and awaits the next volatile addition to reignite the red white and blue bon fire like flames generating economic stimulus and the surgeance of the dollar upward, spreading out the availability of funds so that the lesser off may increase their position to further add wealth to the ever smaller yet further in front percentage perched at the top as the populations multiply to consume modern day necessities long surpassing the basic needs of survival.

Less than a decade after the war Americans owned more cars than the rest of the world combined. Even Will Jr.'s mom, Margaret, had to learn how to drive and obtain a drivers license after the Notts family moved out beyond the end of the line. With alloy improvements still just around the corner surplus war metal afforded the auto manufacturers the ability to produce big and shiny with lots of chrome, and although appearing streamline with the fashionably appealing fins and jet plane overtures the behemoth iron "boats" lacked safety and efficiency which was good for the auto plant workers and scrap yard owners, as well as the oil moguls who transited the truly best use of the U.S. dollar, which was better than any other use of currency in the history of the world....you need it/us (the U.S.) to buy oil! During the right time in history a prudent and ambitious oil futures speculator might easily obtain wealth to get rich in a hurry, practically overnight.

In high school the golden boy, little Will, with his clean complexion and slender build was well liked and popular. The suave only child wasn't nerded out with high grades but was able to cruise through at slightly above average by making up for his somewhat lacking effort with his quick wit, street (or saloon) smarts if you will, and common sense. The handsome hipster played sports well and was allowed to use one of the family cars on a fairly regular basis without unreasonable restrictions from his mom and dad. The naïve rebel side knew how to obtain the occasional alcoholic beverage and locate the current trendy, and generally popular, place to hang out during teen congregation. He went to the prom with his sweetheart the very pretty hazel eyed Ruth Parker. She had a life-long idolizing crush on his savvy shy bad boy image. It was basic textbook history of the fifties into the sixties happily ever after baby boomer viability and growth. In reality the children of this era physically were, with the improved nutrition that was efficiently circulating out to all classes of inhabitants across the country, growing taller, stronger, and healthier than ever before. It was in 1965 that Will Jr. completed his schooling from the newly constructed East Eisenhower High School knowing what it was the acculturated graduate needed to do with next stage of his fated life at this juncture point of his brief maturation.

Vietnam was there calling out to him as the next Korea with the red menace of those commy bastards striving to take control of another subpar scantateous peoples struggling to grow their own way and make it through the developing advancements of the modern world while simultaneously seeking to maintain the culture and heritage of their ancestors. The molded and ripe Will Jr. didn't need to hear it from his father or Uncle Henry, because his innate sense of obligation (which *was* further shaped by their words and tirades) was already there inside of him trumpeting in his thoughts, as if he was back in The Corner Tap listening to their prumptuleous evaluations of the government's policies towards what is needed to obtain and sustain world order and peace to develop prosperity throughout the coming worldwide collaboration and fulfillment of monetary equality. At least that is how it was surmised in the back of his thoughts. As well echoing in the back of his mind were the late president Kennedy's inspirationally patriotic and dutiful obligatory declarations, which were still alive deep down in the thoughts and even sleep of every red blooded loyal American believing in the right over might philosophy of one nation under God, and besides it was the admirably iconic President Kennedy who sent the first troops to the jungles of Vietnam as advisors in the first place.

Unlike many Will Jr. didn't enlist to avoid combat and adverse placement while receiving preferred treatment, nor did the mature teen-ager sham his way through the service. He truly believed he was doing the right thing for his country by executing the examples of honor and nationalism he had picked up and learned at home from his family and environment. The idealistic young adult wanted to do his part and not simply "channel" his life into an unwanted existence or blatantly flee the country like many fearful young men had done. Will's service time was relatively short lived in terms of months. When his unit's position was overrun by NVA the fortunate kid narrowly escaped a nearby RPG explosion with his life. The young enlisted man awoke at MACV thanks to medevac getting his ass out of there in a nick if time. The wounded GI was discharged after spending nearly two months recovering from shrapnel in the back of his leg and Achilles area. There were no souvenirs for him to return to the states with unless if lead in the hamstring and an unwanted and ungratefully received Purple Heart would be considered as war trophies.

By age twenty Will Jr. was back home bitter and drunken, soon to be married to his old high school girlfriend (the now pregnant Ruth Parker), and with a taste for prescription pills would forever walk with a subtle limp somewhat slowing his foot which would drag and scrape slightly along the instep. Eventually as the haggard Will quickly advanced in years the sorrowful leg condition worsened and forced him away from working in the considerably demanding occupation of carpentry, in which the complex romantic loved doing. Yet all the while he always did feel somewhat blessed to be one of the luckier ones to make it back home alive with all of his *physical* parts still there functioning and performing; managing to behave properly for the most part.

It was quite a different return home from reddened battle compared to the one his father and uncle experienced some twenty years earlier. Although Uncle Henry was bitter and sarcastic it never really poisoned the other Vets he was around because there were so many of them around each other and supporting each other as they, the victors over the aggressors, eagerly moved forward towards the unlimited positive and optimistic future times promised to be lying ahead. It is a natural response for disturbing and horrific events, such as the ones Uncle Henry and Will Jr. experienced, to be bothersome and upsetting to a rationally normal person. If one suffers through sights and interactions with catastrophe and death and does not have these bloodied encounters induce a distressing and troubling reaction to them then the individual must not have been sane at the time of the ghastly occurrence in the first place. With little to no adjustment time, Will Jr. was literally fighting in one jungle one day, and with an overnight flight returned to another (the American) jungle the next. When the stressed out veteran was "comfortably' rooted back in his hometown neighborhood, the beliefs and opinions that he witnessed in the community seemed foreign compared to the way the patriotic young citizen had known, remembered, and imagined the spirit of society to be before he ambitiously went off, as well as while the proud and dutiful soldier was gone, half way around the world. Distrust and protest seemed to run rampant and put a clouded veil like film over the whole recollection of existing during those tumultuous times of turmoil, as if memory's wavering vision of nationalism was to be conjured through dense smoke or fog actually resulting in the creation of some fictitious memories in Will's unsettled mind.

Just before Thanksgiving in 1967 Will and his currently ever faithful Ruth joyfully had a son, Jeremiah. While growing up Jeremiah Notts preferred to be called Jeremy simply because the self-conscious boy didn't like his name being associated with the bullfrog song, although later in life, well past adolescence and long after the hit bullfrog song's popularity had ran its course, the more adult Jeremiah grew to appreciate and admire the maturity and virtue of being called by his more distinctive given biblical name of Jeremiah and besides, although everyone may remember those out of place opening lines, the tone and theme of the song quickly switches to another memorable melody praising the new age joy of life on Earth. After all, in the end, your name is the one thing that you own but other people use it more than you do yourself, so it is important to have a good strong healthy name, and be proud of its use and utterance.

Grandpa Notts was ecstatic with the arrival of Jeremiah. Uncle Henry like-wise enjoyed his favorite nephew bringing another Notts man into the world. With younger Will seeming more and more distant to his dad and uncle the new Notts heir was a beam of light for them to shower generous attention upon. Wilbur the senior barely into his fifties seemed to have more energy than his son and although a grandpa was often like a father. The distinguished Will Sr.'s signature military type crew cut was always neatly kept even well into his seventies when it finally had become somewhat gray and thinning. The barber was like a family member to him, a brother, and like another uncle for Jeremy who enjoyed going with his grandpa to get his hair cut at least once a month. The shop was in an ancient art deco baroquely ornate building in the square, and as old as the square itself. When young Jeremy walked in old school original country music would be playing at a level he could barely hear, but was always there buzzing and twanging in the ear. It was low enough for Paul and Joe, the two balding brothers who owned the shop, to spin *their* gospel and gossip while methodically maneuvering their artful clippers, yet still allow the craftsmen to faintly catch the news and weather forecast. The articulated tin ceiling seemed to soar to the sky and the two coiffeurs must have been majestic great hunters when not ardently snipping hair for there were giant moose and elk heads mounted mysteriously to the lofty, barbarously beaming, whitewashed plaster walls, along with numerous other large and small game.

Later Jeremy learned that Paul and Joe also ran a successful taxidermy business when not hunting, fishing, or lowering ears. They often told the influential lad, after they had finished up his trim and sent him on his way, or before he completely departed out the door to the next adventure with Grandpa Notts, "Don't forget to wash behind the ears." When he was an adult, and recalled those early days with his grandfather, the barber's advice created some type of reflection on perhaps there being some type of a hidden meaning in their stern message. Of course it could be taken at face value, after all they were getting a good look back there and a normal energetic growing boy can tend to get some dirt on their hands, face, and hard to reach places where they may hurriedly forget to scrub thoroughly. However, as his mind and thinking matured, he wondered if it meant something deeper which pertained to his thoughts. Your brain is also behind your ears, so to speak, and that is where your thoughts generate from. They could have been suggesting a duel meaning to him. Simply to go about you're your daily life well cleansed, but also to keep your mind free from temptations and not to be desiring ill will and wrongdoing. Scrub those thoughts away and focus on the golden rule and doing that which is right. Either way it often crossed through his mind when anger struck him, or while bathing in the shower.

To Jeremy the barbers knew as much as, if not even more, about things than even Uncle Henry knew about things. Not really connecting it at that young age, down the road he would realize in an epiphany moment that the bartender and barber are actually very similar vocations. Overcoming and seeing through all the shock and awe Jeremy enjoyed journeying to the barbershop with grandpa Notts, not just because he could get some M&M's or salted and shelled peanuts out of the little red candy machine with the glass globe on top by turning the shiny handle which he could hear allowing the dime to magically break up into an overflowing handful of goodies, or because he could mechanically guide a bottle of Green River through the mazy track of the pop cooler, but because Paul or Joe would have him climb up on the chair and treat him like any other customer, consequently making the small boy feel as if he was eighteen years old.

Fighting off the demons tormenting his life Will Jr. struggled through the years of raising his son. Adjustment never really occurred for him. The reintegration process wasn't fully cultivated in time for his utilization and anti-detriment, as later in history the opposite end of the spectrum came full circle where it seemed that the emphasized profit of helping one individual outweighed the value of benefitting society as a whole. His father refused to understand why his only son, who once had the world by the short hairs, couldn't ever get over his battle stress and combat exhaustion, and just move on normally. This only made it more strenuous for Will Jr. The like-minded Uncle Henry on the other hand was more sympathetic and supportive as he recognized that it was a more serious condition like stress response syndrome, but not quite shell shock. Poor health and recession later forced Will Jr. to take a job driving a bakery van which, with its limited physical exertion, eventually led to another unpleasant health issue, that of being overweight.

Needless to say as the years flipped along his marriage wasn't very stable and roughly about the same time in history as such pivotal and essential occurrences as SDI, space shuttle, and ISS initiations, and a couple of years before the famous Reagan Berlin Wall words, yet coinciding with the biggest event from his family's point of view (Jeremy's graduation), divorce was inevitable. In reality it had happened much earlier than the technicality of filing official paperwork. The inspirational Ruth was an eternally kind and honest women in addition to being a highly dedicated parent. While still in her thirties, even if just barely, it was good for her to move on and become happy with her faithful and submissive devoted life of obedience before it woefully passed her by. The beautiful and smart lovely lady later would acceptably and vibrantly remarry proceeding to respectfully afterword give birth to Jeremiah's stepsister Amada, which would consequently rekindle spirited ambitions put aside long ago.

Often questioning the meaning of his life, as well as life itself, Will Jr.'s appearance was at times out of place or homeless looking. In a severe state of stupor the scraggly "Nome" type man might babble things like "bomb everything" or "bomb Disneyland" in some type of timeless dark remembrance of a distant ordeal. Drinking and pills really took a hard toll on the troubled veteran's tortuous life. Fit wise his breathing was extremely labored from years of chain smoking and exposure to toxic inhalants while working in construction unprotected on commercial remodeling sites before more strongly enforced OSHA regulations were adhered to.

To Will Jr. there never seemed to be a hazardous health threat with smoking as he grew up in a period with no warning labels and where co-existence around the common place and acceptance of smoking was the indeterminable norm. Pile the kids into the station wagon, without seatbelts or car seats, everyone over sixteen light up, and cruise down the country roads at seventy-five miles per hour. If there were any complaints from disobedient young family members reach back and smack them firmly with the back of the hand and, if really out of line, the belt when back at home. How any children of that era made it into adulthood still seems a miracle.

It wouldn't be until the late 1970's early 1980's (after most of the damage was done to Will Jr. who wouldn't be quitting his sinful self-indulgent habits in his lifetime), that anti-smoking campaigns began popping up in civilization, although not actually taking a well heeded foothold until much much later, till it was eventually perceived almost as evil by an ever changing fickle culture practically lynch mobbish. In the early stages of covert citizen control, through steering the public perception, advertisement laws became much more restrictive for tobacco (and alcohol products as well), till packaging of these vices which were bad for people's health would need to contain dire health warnings to the point, well down the line, where do-gooders wanted to have no advertising whatsoever and all plain labeling with only a Skull & Cross bones next to the deadly warning declaration. More than likely some alcohol or tobacco companies also had an incalculable controlling interest in some type of media outlet or news publication where they wanted the process to proceed at the speed of ocean rise or the moon slipping away. As Hollywood actors such as Yule Brenner spoke out against smoking, it wouldn't be surprising that those being adversely effected were paying other movie stars to be seen smoking in public. There was the original poster child shriveled up "elderly" woman shock deterrent speaking to the populace through a tube with the words "smoking is glamorous," gurgling overhead. No smoking in restaurants, no smoking in public places, no smoking indoors, no smoking electronic cigarette devices indoors or in public places, and the cost of one pack taxed to be equal to or more than working an hour at minimum wage all should clean up society's act. Unfortunately there still is the poor bar maid who never dropped a dime on a single smoke in her whole life but gets nose cancer either second hand from work or third hand from the furnished apartment she moved into or the used car she bought, but don't completely stop accommodating smokers all together because they still will make up a percentage of a business's patronage to contribute to their bottom line.

The once young, prospectful, and domineering Will Jr. continued to drive the lightly taxing bread route until 1993 when his longtime health issues finally physically prevented him from working productively, consequently officially disabling him at a relatively young age. Straining to breath and struggling to walk, the last two putrid years of his unfulfilled existence were predominately spent in a wheelchair, or a seated forearm exerciser as the low spirited self-blaming drunk would lightly refer. The concerned doctors tried and wanted to do more for the haggard Will Jr., but the morose vet was running out of steam and unmeasurably didn't care to go to, or put in the effort to, schedule appointments. It was easier for the Gloomy Gus to drink, smoke, and sulk. Fundamentally leery of doctors the untrusting cynic credulously believed that somehow, when he was opened up for each of the numerous surgeries being executed inside of him, disease and additional sickness, suffering, and affliction would endlessly spread un-wholesomely throughout his entire body further crippling him and ultimately shortening his life span; as if that actually mattered to the hopelessly surrendered soul burning out inside of the shallow shadow precipitated by the man's past virility which once shined brightly through.

Finally, just before the looming panic of the upcoming fear of a Y2K collapse, in November of 1999, Wilbur Notts Jr. gave way to "congestive heart failure." Drowning himself in self-pity and regret while believing that he was a bad role model to his clean and uncorrupted son, Will ultimately was never able to see how his careless and obstinate behavior actually had an extremely profound and positive influence in cultivating his son's growth through life. Sometimes the poorest example can actually become the best. From an example of what not to do when troubles and adversity plague and disturb your daily development Jeremiah would ripen into a respected member of the community contributing good will and generosity to those in need of help and support; almost, as if in a sense of actualization, fulfilling where his father's potential might have taken him after high school had the circumstances been different. While sorrowful the nearly seventy-five year old energetic and witted, ever devoted, Will Sr. forever felt a responsibility to be there for, look after, and season his fatherless grandson, and thus made a full hearted effort to be available to play a bigger role in any upcoming times of need in Jeremiah's maturing life.

Growing up for Jeremiah Notts wasn't always smooth sailing. There were bumps in the road. Though the death of his father was hard on all the members of the Notts clan there was a positive sense of relief and comfort to everyone for Will Jr., believing that just maybe the troubled Will Jr. might finally be liberated and at peace. Even so no amount of condolence could ever erase or ease the fact that this was still his dad that had just passed away at only fifty-two years of age.

Eight years before the mortal death of his father, in July of 1991, Jeremy endured the loss of the beloved, 69 year old, Uncle Henry. This sad event occurred roughly one month before the date set and anticipated for the young man's wedding and marriage to the gorgeous Danica Marshall. Needless to say this put a bit of a damper on what was supposed to be the biggest celebration, and happiest day, to this point, of their fresh, new fledged blossoming lives together. Everyone attempted to have fun at the wedding and spoke in the highest regard in great recognition about the life of the very well-liked Uncle Henry, pushing back the sadness of the funeral which seemed like it just happened the day before. Thinking of postponing the wedding was briefly considered, but it just didn't seem possible after over a year of preparation and besides every one truly believed that Uncle Henry surely would have been the first to demand the momentous event to go on as planned. Sort of as in honor of Uncle Henry, and to pay a last respect and farewell, they all took a somber reminisceful trip to the old neighborhood to raise a glass to Uncle Henry, and have a drink in remembrance of him at The Corner Tap. When they arrived there the early 20th century dingily pollution stained yellow common brick building with its detailed stone façade was in the process of being torn down while the rest of the lot and entire block were being cleared away. There was a large wooden sign mounted on 4X4 posts extending from the ground with an artistic rendering of some new complex painted onto it and reading: "future sight of Canopy Corners Condominiums." It all shows that one thing is for certain. Change is always constantly occurring on a timeless and endless course, instantaneously molding everything that is boundlessly strung together.

There were also times in Jeremy's youth when normal adolescent straying called for parental reprimand. One instance was being returned to The Corner Tap on a Saturday afternoon by a police officer for running in front of cars and stirring up other types of trouble outside the tavern after telling Grandpa Notts and Uncle Henry that he was going to the candy store with the dollar of saved up allowance money he had in his pocket. Luckily the two matured brothers were friends with Butch, (Officer Davis), so the kid's punishment was to sit quietly by himself in a corner booth with no soda only a glass of water to drink, and all he was allowed to do was read from the stack of Sgt. Rock comic books he had brought with from home. The sternness of Officer Davis, coupled with the interactions of the being apprehended encounter itself, left the young Jeremiah temporarily scared into rehabilitation and determined to go on the straight and narrow. Later after his shift had finished up Officer Davis returned to The Corner Tap and sat in Jeremy's jail cell of a booth to have a man to man talk with the pouty youngster. It was actually Grandpa Notts and Uncle Henry who deserved to be reprimanded for not taking time away from their marathon card games to pay better attention to what types of mischief might evolve from the energy and curiosity of an enthusiastic and developing ten year old mind yearning for excitement and new knowledge. Maybe for punishment Officer Davis could have chained the two old timers to the basement floor and forced them to eat stale peanuts and drink flat beer.

During a similar time of his influential maturation young Jeremiah was caught by his outraged mother for both stealing and smoking. Mrs. Notts, Ruth, heard two boys outside coughing unhealthily and wondered what on Earth they could be choking on and immediately suspected cigarettes. Talk about being caught red handed, or green faced ready to throw up would be more accurate. Jeremy and his best friend Mike Tomms seemed to just have too much time on their hands over summer vacation. There they were sitting on the teal colored cast iron bench set into the lava rock alongside the back of the house with their baseball gloves on one hand while puffing away on the plastic tipped cigars, Tiparillos, with their free hand. Ironically one of the baseball gloves actually *was* dyed red. When the ill-behaved boys realized that they were just about to be caught they tried to hastily hide the cancer sticks in their mitts, but it was too late. Jeremy's outraged mother was on top of them instantaneously and irritable yelped, "Where did you boys get these?" The shameful Jeremy reluctantly replied, "The drug store up town." Mike didn't say one word and tried to sneak away from the extremely pissed off Mrs. Notts who this time barked out, "Who bought these for you?" At this point Mike was overwhelmingly tempted to just make a break for it and sprint straight home. This was even scarier than being led by the arm into The Corner Tap by Officer Davis.

Finally it all came out how Jeremy watched for the store clerks while Mike slipped them into his sock while pretending to tie his shoe. The boys had become intrigued by a Johnny Bench commercial where the all-star catcher says "take a tip, smoke Tiparillos." The little cigars looked cool and seemed sophisticated, but man how they could make a pre-teen sick to the stomach. Mike was commanded home as Ruth called his mother and filled her in on the disappointing details. The two concerned and upset mothers wondered what might be next. Maybe spray paint tagging, or even worse, sniffing, with "no drips, no runs, no errors," another Bench commercial this time promoting spray paint. Not in these mom's lifetimes if they had anything to say and do about it.

Jeremiah got his ass healthily spanked for starters, and then grounded for the rest of the summer to stay out of any further trouble. All of this and more, and Ruth didn't even know about the Saturday afternoon incident at The Corner Tap with Grandpa Notts and Uncle Henry. In addition to being grounded Jeremy was also to use his allowance money from chores to pay back the cost of five boxes of Tiparillos, forfeiture of any allowance money left, and a six month suspension of upcoming allowance money. A sincere face to face apology, along with a hand written one, were to be delivered to Mr. Barry, the drug store manager, accompanying the payment for the unknown number of stolen Tiparillos. Throughout the rest of his childhood years Jeremy devotedly succeeded to sincerely stay out of trouble at home and in school. As a pragmatic high schooler his grades were exceptionally good and he never complained about any duties or responsibilities delegated around the house. Besides later smashing the front end on his mom's car into a tree when the antilock brakes failed the novice motorist on a rainy evening during early driving years, this was the last of Jeremiah's wrong doing and the later fender incident was really only a slight mishap as the distracted driving charges were dutifully dismissed by the DA.

Four year college isn't for everyone after graduation. Jeremiah's SAT and ACT scores were above average enough to allow him an extensive number of colleges to choose from but after experimenting with higher education for two semesters he decided to try a different route and found himself learning the HVAC trade. The heating and air-conditioning life seemed a good fit for the handy and proficient young man whose analytical integral mind easily derived that, after all, those *are* two things difficult to live without in the modern world. Even through the early 21st century housing gludge and prolonged recession where his annual income was substantially less than during the booming times before the mortgage crackdown and home value correction, cold spells and heat waves kept him, as well as most hacks, fairly busy. It was an honest living with relatively steady pay to later support his new marriage and fledgling family. This was a good thing because not long after Jeremiah's marriage to Danica they were with child. About two years after the ADA took effect, which at that point was a little too late to be beneficial for the crass Uncle Henry, who on his last legs, would sarcastically say to his "buddies", from his final bed at the VA hospital, "what do those panty wastes need all that special treatment for anyway." Also coincidentally coinciding about the same time El Nino was first smacking off the parched lips of West Coasters, in December 1992, the newest Mr. and Mrs. Notts received an early Christmas gift, their son Matthew Notts. This seemed to bring a fresh outlook for the future of the ever optimistic Notts clan, the sour Uncle Henry now departed.

Jeremiah's HVAC mentor, Roy Sanders, took the youthful, ambitious, and energetic Jeremiah, who followed more after Grandpa Notts than his own dad, (Will Jr.), under his wing and whole heartedly taught him the everlasting skillful ins and outs of the profession as if Jeremiah was his own son. Actually only a short time after being introduced to the divorced mother of the motivated and enthusiastic Jeremiah, Roy would marry Ruth making Jeremiah truly his son, his step-son. The two divorcees hit it off naturally together and would live out the rest of their lives nearly inseparable. The newly-weds oopsy daughter together, the big eyed and kinky haired Amanda, would be Jeremiah's step-sister and the newborn Matt Notts' aunt only a slight bit his elder, making them more like cousins.

Matt Notts was born into the world old enough to remember what he was doing on that infamous day when the fueled-up jet airplanes were used as bombs and guided into the ill-fated buildings they devastated and dusted in an explosive crash. He could also remember the funeral of his grandfather, Wilbur Notts Jr., just before turning seven in 1999. Matt was not quite a digital native, but on the cusp. Any one born before 2000 was of course a digital immigrant yet the "digital" era was there available to Matt at an early age and so he did well to blend in knowing the manipulation of the devices, which would play an everyday role proceeding limitlessly into the future, while he was growing up. This was the blended age where digital immigrants blended with the anxious Millennials and socially inept digital natives till eventually one day nearly everyone would be born into, or at least assimilated into, as part of the modern anti-clandestine cyber generations; this of course until some new designations are coined to describe the certain upcoming future generation gaps.

The new millennium's days churned into existence just the same as any other year trudges forward. Grinding away down the timeline there was no immediate asteroid strike at midnight, or a rapture event beaming people up to heaven, nor city sized space ships controlled by the lost ancestors of Atlantis living in a hollow Earth beneath the poles bringing good will along with Vrillian knowledge and enlightenment to reveal the hidden powers of the human mind and solve all the world's problems for us. The poles didn't flip over overnight on 12-21-12 either, and unfortunately for those end of the world phobics there was no biological extermination of mankind in 2016, or the nuclear annihilation in 2020. There was no Hitlerian mass decapitation of Christian heads to lead to the rule of the yellow race. Just as always a new world born each and every day, slowing absorbing into and adapting to the future with a new approach to old problems with fresh terms for the same ole characters. Terrorists and evil doers committing mass murder and chaos, leaving a hint of doubt for safety during everyday life in the back of everyone's mind. Not much different than Oklahoma City, the Twin Towers toppling down were just another enactment of cowardly jealous anger raising awareness but not preventing future despicable and tragic undertakings, such as the Dallas Dirty Bomb, the Chechnya Pulsar, or the July 5th Sunrise Attacks, from unfortunately occurring on a somewhat routinely regular basis across the globe.

In the ages of instant communication it was essential for a person to really watch their P's and Q's and be careful not to mention any type of unlawful action or discriminatory bias, even in the feeblest fragment of dry humor or that person could find themselves in court facing serious charges of espionage, terrorism, hate, or even treason. Threats *were* taken seriously and investigated by the NSA industriously. Speaking out wasn't as simple as crooning out the sarcastic stanzas of an 80's Punk Rock song. Offensive and anti-government lyrics could be the subject of censorship and litigation, sometimes even in rap music. Citizens also needed to be careful in public not to conjure trouble from the ACLU by inadvertently offending any protected classes or minority groups (which include and involve the majority of the people), nor make any reckless actions, even if only in the slightest bit of casual nonconformist rebellion or over-spirited juvenile mischief, because there could at any time be someone lurking unseen in the shadows covertly recording indiscriminate whimsical actions with some type of device that they were attached to as closely as the joint mapping sensors of a tele-operated, thought controlled, cybernetic robotic prosthetic. But with all the loose nut loonies going postal or off the deep end, in some type of snapping killing spree, how could anyone or society be over safe. You just never know who the next walk into a school and kill children mentally incapacitated individual will be so society can never be too safe, although the turmoil is still going to happen no matter what procedures and preventive measures the government, as well as watch groups and concerned citizens, try to implement and laws and cameras and other deterrents are deployed. As drones are continuously hovering overhead mapping a farm field's season or checking the progress of freeway repairs, as well as the other security monitors which were quietly watching the intersections and vestibules, high resolution satellites were stealthily observing and examining the four corners of the Earth for suspicious activities and non-conformists as humanity proceeded to the future, one minute with rights then suddenly the next minute with limited rights, or even penitently one could find themselves martyrized haplessly and to be without any rights altogether.

Matt was not quite eleven when he got his first experience using a cellular phone. Skateboarding next to his slightly older buddy, Drew, who was on his lightning bolt adorned hand-me-down roller blades, the duo noticed that the portly neighbor Mrs. Jennings had left her passenger window more than half down as her emerald green Pontiac Bonneville SSE sat parked parallel to the curb. Passing alongside the piece of a car the two curious carousers noticed an enticing flip phone resting unattended on the passenger seat. The temptation to practice adulthood seemed to outweigh the consequences of where their actions might lead them. Envisioning yourself doing and making the right choices is easier than the difficulty of following through with the actuality of what is right. Needless to say the inexperienced inquisitive criminals circled back and wheeled off with the archaic communicator. Just before needing to be home for supper they stopped off at the playground of the lush Sunset Park where a couple of Matt's nerdy classmates were slowly spinning on the merry-go-round just a short distance from the paved basketball hoops they rolled up on. While Matt and Drew were pretending to make calls as if they were businessmen conducting important transactions the grubby play grounders inconspicuously meandered over to the court to get into the action.

Who to call was the biggest question. One of the dorks blurted out, "let's call China." Taking charge, Drew said that they would call 911 and say that there was a fire, lie back, and watch the firemen come. O.K., but first Matt needed to call home and tell his mom where he was and when he would be home. Of course none of this would work. They needed to come up with a better plan.

"Let's order a pizza to that brown house across the street and watch what happens when they show up," was uttered seemingly from the sky above. Matt would just have to forget about getting home at normal time and worry about explaining himself later.

When the compact yet sporty red four-door with the lighted magnetic Pizza Hut placard on the roof showed up to the un-expecting ranch home, nearly within ear shot of the echoing Sunset Park, and the driver got out carrying a stack of pizza boxes, the mischievous rascals pretended to go about their usual play. The two geeks on the merry-go-round were sluggishly circulating while Matt and Drew were rolling deliberately snailed across the pavement nonchalantly observing the awkward encounter unfolding across the street. It was good play for them and they all went home jittery apprehensive with the satisfaction of knowing they pulled off a successful prank in cahoots with each other, almost like a team.

The battery in the nascent electronic archetype quickly ran out from numerous calls and low resolution video games, but Drew was able to find a charger that would plug into the opening on the side allowing the delinquent boys to get away with using the cell phone for a day or two more, calling their friends, and pulling off a couple of additional minor dupes as well as several more crank calls, forever being sure not to answer when someone was calling, most likely to locate the "misplaced" early and primitive, yet classical, personal interactive networking aide, (PINA), which at that time was mainly used for verbal communication and assisting complimentary exchange with minimal information interaction and linkage, but still a valued individual diagnostic attachment as a crucial contact connection companion as well as a helpful acquaintance advocate mechanism.

When Matt and his cronies were finally found out only a few days later, he had to promise never to do it again and give an apology to the voluptuous fat lady telling her that he was sorry, while Matt's mother, Danica, wrote Mrs. Jennings a check for $300 to cover the excessive phone charges. Drew on the other hand, there wasn't much hope for. He was always going to be a troublesome kid and it really wasn't much longer before he and Matt grew further and further apart till in adult life where they never saw each other again. Drew was on his way towards a life time of misguided behavior.

Eventually Matt would hear about Drew in the news as a City Transit Authority worker getting arrested for credit card skimming. The irony was how he complained about so many of the cards being maxed out too close to their limit. How that screw-up ever got a job with the CTA is beyond Matt's belief, but the fact that he was a CTA employee was why it made the news allowing Matt to hear of the crime, and Drew for the last time. After years of growing apart, and leading different lives, it wasn't as if the misfit would have ever gotten invited to Matt's wedding, or anything else for that matter, anyhow.

It was actually quite some time before Matt in fact did finally marry. It seemed Matt would either be dating a nice goody-two-shoes girl or a hoe bag. He would wish the wholesome girl to be a little more risqué and the naughty miss to be a bit more virginal. It would take a while to find the happy medium. His particularness could be why he waited so long to get married although getting married later in life was more and more common than say in Grandpa Notts' day. Being more established and financially secure to raise a family, or even just have a moderate household, was the wise choice of many apprehensive and uncertain vacillating couples with aspirations of pursuing professional careers where establishment is frugally and dutifully put ahead of suffering through a life of financial hardships and struggles.

Living the ideal slacker existence at home while working at a cultivation center, Matt was nearly thirty before he finally decided to quit burning up time, pack it up, and ditch the nest. It wasn't until after meeting the red-haired light of his life, the highly educated Amber, who had a budding professional career as an Orthodontist and was a couple of years older, but miles more mature, before he ultimately realized that maybe it did make sense to roll over a new leaf, fix his act, straighten up and fly right, instead of zig-zagging aimlessly through the puffy and pleasant green grasses of life.

2008 was a sorrowful and grief stricken year for the altruistic Grandpa Notts. His beloved wife and companion (to simply use the word wife does not full describe a daily relationship of more than sixty years, as there really are not words that can accurately explain and illustrate in a way to appropriately conjure a visualization of a lifelong bond such as theirs), Margaret, or Grandma Notts, at age 83 passed away peacefully one warm fall afternoon in a quiet room of St. Alexis Hospital from pneumonia complications leaving a deep ravine of sadness in the generous heart of her surviving soul mate, Wilbur.

Not so much directly related to the engraven anguish felt by Grandpa Notts, but extremely sad and mournful all the same during that grief-stricken year, was the tragic death of the son of Jeremiah's childhood friend Mike Tomms. The death of Mason Tomms was a type of collateral damage of the addiction to the technological craze controlling the anxiety of self fulfillment in the youth as well as in the adults lacking the gratification of where their life has led. Becoming distracted was one of the biggest drawbacks of early mobile communication and information devices, people just can't walk and chew gum, or text and listen to music, at the same time. Being injured or killed by a train in an urban area from distracted walking wasn't as uncommon as one might think. What was more strange was the fact that a hearing impaired teenager was shot and killed only a week earlier while standing unsuspecting, and unaware of posing any type of threat or menace, on that exact same platform. The signing gestures made by the innocent child were mistaken for the flashing of gang signs. Maybe the movements were actually somewhat similar in mimicking affiliation motions, but to be blamelessly gunned down was a drastic and sadly sardonic commonality, expressing only the harshness of civilization.

The real kicker for Grandpa Notts wasn't the passing of his beloved elderly wife or the accidental death of the child of an acquaintance he had only been briefly introduced to, but, out of the blue, only a short time later, his special grandson, the cherished Jeremiah, came to a sudden unforeseen end after just turning forty-one prior to the winter holidays. Once again the everlasting Grandpa Notts was left as the one surpassing everyone else to devotedly and respectfully oversee, attend, and suffer through the services and burial of yet another loved one to pass on ahead of him, and be put in the ground before their time, in this occurrence making the pre-adult Matt, his only blood heir left to carry on the family line, and to become the man of the household, looking after and being there for his never to remarry mother, Danica, whom consequently, Matt had always had an exceptionally close relationship with.

It was very difficult on the vivacious Danica Notts to lose her husband so young and swift. To her it seemed just the day before they had their whole future together drawn out and lingering ahead of them. One day there is a mention of a slight head-ache and the next Jeremiah is in the hospital hooked up to beeping machines with tubes poking into his pale skin and drab green display screens monitoring every pulse generated from his frail, worn down, and suffering body; brain dead. No choice but to cut the line and hopefully some of the middle aged man's body parts may be harvested and used to benefit the life of some broken down and deteriorating individual in need of a donation of replacement organs.

As Jeremiah's lifelong best friend Mike Tomms completed the all-embracing performance of the heart felt and tear jerked eulogy recounting their brother-like relationship (which was understandably unable to justly answer with any logical reasoning the impossible to rationalize), Danica justified in her head that if matter cannot be created or destroyed, and humans are ashes to ashes dust to dust, then everything a person consumes and extracts as waste turns back into part of the planet. As the sphere of our planet is a steady fluctuation of a constant mass and Jeremiah's flesh and bones decay to keep the Earth's essence in equilibrium, balancing out the air we breathe with the dust we leave, she was left feeling a sense that she would still be close to him, being around his spirit through the beautiful constant core of nature and the putative luminiferous aethereal energy of the universe. This theosophical esotericism left her content to believe their immortal human magnetism might join again on a future etheric plane, glowing divine together through the monadic progression of the unknown root of mankind's journey through the laws of periodicity and cyclicity ever enhancing the eternal soul.

There were numerous suitors in pursuit of the beautiful widow, however she had a difficult time giving in and connecting. There were early life experiences preventing her from trusting, bonding, and freeing herself. A large part of Danica's identity was connected and tied to her life with her late husband which created a feeling for her that she would forever be, and be known as, Jeremiah's wife.

After the unexpected and abrupt death of his father Matt spent a lot of time being tutored and mentored by the flamboyant Grandpa Notts who was a young and ageless mid-eighties, as if for him eighty was the new sixty. Plain and simply, at eighty-four Grandpa Notts was an everlasting survivor, and a damn good one at that. Matt became very close to his great grandfather who was more than willing to use his keen mind to inundate the perplexed wet around the ears teenager with the many feats of his colorful life. Sharing his wealth of life long experienced insight and wisdom as well as advisement from lustrous accomplishments, he taught the boy the value of keeping your head up through hardship and adversity, and to always be optimistic to a smooth, calm, and bright future ahead, because you don't ever know what good may be in store for you even if at the time things are overwhelmingly not going well and there are rough conditions pulling you down trying to engulf you. He would say to the youngster in a fluid religious like tone, "When one door closes on you another shall open." Maybe *that* was the logic and philosophy behind the continuing optimism throughout his lengthened lifetime and enduring tenure.

One of the red, white, and blue Grandpa Notts' favorite activities of enlightenment was to bring Matt along to the VFW for a hot lunch (and occasional fashion show). Knowing the kid's situation the volunteers and workers, as well as the patrons, would look the other way at his baby faced presence there, and even on occasion allow him to have a short glass of beer to share with his great-grandfather, Major Notts, as the aged crafty and artistic story teller recounted countless dazzling tales of astonishment, frequently being sure not to leave out the startling wonder of Uncle Henry as well as other memorable and cherished details of family history. Even though Grandpa Notts never came anywhere close to the rank of Major, for some reason at the VFW that was how they referred to the ageless and antiquated gentleman, being in such a way in which he seemed to thoroughly endear and enjoy. Matt's dad, Jeremiah, although not a veteran himself, would frequently donate some of the precious free time he once had, to help out with special events and fund raisers set up by the VFW. Needless to say his presence there, as well as in his philanthropic work with other charitable organizations he was actively involved with in the community, were benevolent behaviors of his to be substantially missed. There was a strong Notts tie there, in the VFW, through years of service, membership, and contribution. There were many photos displayed on the walls showing Grandpa Notts, Uncle Henry, and Will Jr. in scenes of fun and humor, as well as engaged in serious business.

Matt's time of innocence flashed by in the blink of an eye. The natural narcissism of normal teen-age temperament continued into early adult years and at times he could be a bit of a stooge; ungracious and selfish. The slow to mature selfist felt that he didn't owe the world anything and that it was only there to satisfy his desires. Expending little appreciation the self-centered materialist was born into an era where many of the youth wanted and expected all of the world's lavishes and joys to just be there for them to have fun with, without wasting effort for attainment, nor exercising any desire to be grateful, give back, or share. It was as if the guidance and advice of Grandpa Notts fell onto deaf ears and the altruistic old man's constructive influence wasn't taken to heart. Secretly deep down, during this self-seeking point of his growth and development, Matt earnestly contemplated and awaited the passing of Grandpa Notts looking to receive and counting on inheritance, which he felt was money that could be put to the best use contributing to the gratification of himself. This outlook and rationale of insolence of course was prior to his meeting of Amber and the loss of his mother and aunt.

The irony was that one of Grandpa Notts and Uncle Henry's most legendary and timeless everyday sayings, way back at The Corner Tap after the war, was, "It's only money." For them to be safely and securely back home with family, friends, and the peace of mind of not having to be troubled and concerned, stressing and agonizing, about being taken out by a bullet or a bomb, was their greatest wealth. Grandpa Notts surely would have given Matt any amount in which he could obtain to hand down to the last of his lineage, barring the selling of his home or now collector plated Lincoln, which seldom left the garage as the long lived full of life patriarch approached one hundred.

"Willy Notts" was engraved onto the gold plaque embedded into the instrument panel of the aqua blue 1976 Lincoln Continental Mark IV Givenchy edition which was treasured by the proud Grandpa Notts. The designer series with its white landau vinyl roof was a cherry classic driven in numerous parades as well as showcased at several VFW sponsored events such as swap meets and car shows. The two door coupe he did the once in a lifetime splurge on was the most prized material possession ever owned by the unmaterialistic and laid back Grandpa Notts. At the time when he bought the extravagant indulgence new, and had his own name engraved into the personalized modern custom, he had hoped that it would one day pass down to Will Jr., but sometimes life does not play out the way you think it might or wish it to.

Matt, while driving a human controlled motor vehicle (HCMV) near dusk in his late twenties, dropped his black smart phone when retrieving an e-mail, and hurt some kids sort of badly. In order to be directly accountable and raise enough money to make good on the punitive damages assigned to his ignorant and irresponsible actions the self-absorbed shyster had to sell, piece by piece on the primal auction site known as E-bay, the extensive and exquisite exhibit of Uncle Henry's classic collection of beer cans that were handed down to him as a type of family heirloom representing a by gone age referencing a fulfilled life at The Corner Tap. This was easier than working off the compensation and exhausting the resources he did have available to himself, as these funds were for fun stuff. Mom kicked in the remainder amount Matt wasn't able to produce, this after paying for the best lawyer team available. In reality he got off somewhat easily with a simple monetary judgment and a short amount of probation time, in addition to the increased rates he would have to endure with the high risk insurance after a brief suspension of his license. The injured parties and their relatives were rightfully upset with the somewhat apparent leniency of the court.

The venerable Grandpa Notts could have set him straight, but at this point in his life he was pretty much kept in the dark and just pacified by being fed blissful news to the end of his days. The senior Notts was led to believe Matt was the perfect young gentleman, ideal to proudly and respectfully carry on the image and reputation of his descendants. There was no need in distressing the hoary utopian, or chance wounding his aging bodily conditions with uncertainties about family perception and honor, even though physically Grandpa Notts still seemed to be more fit than many of the much younger gym members who were also working out at his local fitness center doing cardio on the elliptical, treadmill, or exercise bike. In reality more people like "Major" Notts was what the world needed and the value of their insight shouldn't be suppressed and ignored but nurtured and followed to help civilization know what will be in store as history eternally inevitably repeats itself in cyclic fashion.

As the 21ˢᵗ century waxed and waned onward the common place of weather irregularities and dangers burst out more and more erratic and explosive. Tornadoes became no less intense. They began reaching up into the atmosphere sprouting debris balls up to three miles into the sky allowing the immense twisters to be tracked by Doppler radar which was a new phenomenon that hadn't previously occurred way up at 15,000 feet. NOAA SPC sent out PDS (particularly dangerous situation) warnings to inhabitants in the path of these cyclones thousands of feet wide, but an F-4, or even F-3 on the Fujita scale released in the early 1970's, worked like giant vacuum cleaners and then sent the damaging debris balls crashing back down into hospitals, schools, or even jails, whatever was in their unforgiving indiscriminate path. When the cyclogenesis reached the occasional F-5 everyone nearby needed to take serious shelter. In the middle part of the 21ˢᵗ century's first decade an enhanced Fujita scale (EF0-EF5) came out to chronical a better approximation of wind speed and damage based on the years of statistical evaluation. As populations filled in more and more rural areas the odds of escape from hearing of a local weather tragedy became less and less likely, coinciding with the availability of instantaneous information which made disasters immediately known, reaching the point where they virtually became mundane. The debris ball's radar recognition actually allowed a little more time to send out alarm, but how much time is there really to out run a tornado if precariously caught in its undiscerning path?

During the twenty teens and twenty twenties weather really started to get destructive and deadly, beyond just its normal spasmodic seasonal skirmishes. As the weather patterns were in the beginning stages of their unheeded and previously ignored cyclical shift, intemperate and irregular systems would tend to get stuck over a specific stretch, causing one region to experience record documented drought while another nearby is being inundated with vast amounts of rainfall and catastrophic flooding, or historical heat would occur one year then acute cold the next. A changing atmospheric make-up fueled the effects of the extreme swings, as global warming and climate change, words which were previously adapted into culture, were finally seriously reaching mainstream acknowledgement and flowing into fruition full force to fabricate and form the normal weather affinity befalling most people in one manner or another, either being temperature, precipitation, or a peculiar climatic outburst such as a haboob blowing blinding dust across an arid state.

PDS alerts released by the NWS were more and more frequent till they were almost like the familiar everyday air raid siren of WWII England. Tornados would even pop up out of season from brewing winter windstorms as powerful clippers, blasts, and vortexes streamed down from the poles. A micro-burst could spring up in a fast moving seasonal storm scurrying across the states to rip up trees and break over light poles and street lights, while rogue winds could blast through for minutes at a time to uproot any unassuming obstacles situated in its zone (RWZ).

As each season, year, and decade continuously pass proceeding monotonously to the future, the tracking and study of meteorological activity and behavior graph a broader picture through collective data accumulation and analytical pattern studies for improved formulation of beneficial planetary weather understanding. Some environmental risks and natural conditions go hand in hand. For swimmers and sun worshippers Beach Hazard warnings can drift red to green on a daily basis depending on atmospheric activity. Oil spill devastations or toxic waste leakage may be slowed, or worsened, by the Earth's innate defense mechanisms or its timelessly cultivated daily cycling procedures. Either way FEMA wanted every individual to be prepared and supplied for any and all spontaneous perils, being either a man made or induced calamity, or a naturally occurring ecological upheaval or cataclysm.

Shortly before meeting Amber and not long after hocking Uncle Henry's beer can collection Matt faced a pivotal hardship of his own. A ten inch deluge in addition to a week of steady spring rains caused the banks of a nearby river to overflow in what was called a one hundred year flood. Much of the town was damaged beyond repair as the local community would require a vast amount of government relief funds to rebuild. The basement palace in which the thriving bachelor lavishly presided was all but ruined. After losing all of the Earthly possessions in which he had accumulated over the years of his trivial existence, and seeing the anguish of his devastated hometown surroundings, Matt finally realized that maybe there were more important things to value in life, and the World didn't revolve around himself. On a personal level, after this trying test of character, Matt's immaturity and self-centered principles justly vanished.

He for once needed to be strong for real, and this is when he finally became grown up and responsible. He was now appreciative to the frailty of life.

From a middle aged point of view, Matt was barely into his thirties at the time that **One** of the worst outbreaks to unharmoniously balance the build-up of life on Earth is believed to have first occurred on a clear and cold star lit night when a fast moving, unforeseeable icy raw, billion year old, heavenly space rock came from the primal undisturbed depths of the cosmos (most likely from the Kuiper belt at the edge of our solar system), and silently blasted through the planet's atmosphere. A cosmic air burst crashing unnoticed into a Far Eastern pristine mountainside to release extremophiles and primitive unrefined organic building blocks patiently waiting for the right biological circumstances to hatch as an NPMR, newborn progressive macrobiotic reaction.

Due to its remote impact site, the crater itself wasn't immediately located by the Sherpa guides escorting the scientific research expedition above the timberline. It was however pin-pointed in the ideal spot for the preliminary flu-like symptoms to hitch a ride up into the jet stream while prevailing wind currents spread the respiratory menace methodically down wind. The initial introductory break-up in the atmosphere, which actually *was* detected by satellite imagery, is believed to be what caused the accumulative reddish colored precipitation to superstitiously drizzle alongside the sparse altitudes dropping sprinkling flurries that dusted the unwitting environment and led to the naming of Red Rain Respiratory Syndrome, or 3RS as it was universally known. Shortly after the recognition of this new sickness was finally accepted, lakes near the primeval Earthly introduction containing toxic algae, that contaminated drinking water and choked plantation, would later be linked to this original and rudimentary 3RS occurrence by the Center for Infectious Disease.

Traversing the globe with teleportation like speed, flus and viruses could spread further and faster than ever before. The enveloping effect of the Earth's rotation sailing and spreading the air, along with modern global travel simplicity, allowed 3RS to fly along and easily jump from continent to continent. The Super El Nino the following year didn't help with slowing the circulation of the germinal disorder, which spread around the world at a lethargic "unassuming" rate. By the time the first death occurred it was estimated the one millionth person was getting symptoms and inadvertently passing the festering bacteria along to others. No amount of hand sanitizer or FDA cleared particulate masks were going to stop this pathogenic biological air borne pestilence from seeking out its victims. Notice and action just weren't taken fast enough as the fatal ailment was later coined the sleeping flu, because at first the noxious malady would lay dormant only showing common cold characteristics which quickly went away leaving a brief false sense of safety, thus being mistakenly disregarded. It wouldn't be till months later that the dots could connect back to 3RS.

It was the 21st century's Spanish Flu, Black Death, or Justinian Plague. Near its initial Earthly invasion 3RS flowed down the gushing spring time rapids flushing out into the air through the frothing whirlpools translucent with a yellowish hew, leaving behind the bio-invader which was an interloper taking root in the not so rich jungle soil. A murky colony festering in a fizzing foggy steam, which after prolonged ingestion is as noxious as an acidic sulfur mustard like gas reminiscent of the first Great War. A low lying murderer leaching of the oxygen in the water creating pools that are lacking the bland featureless basic element it has been stripped of and thus rendering the surrounding soil somewhat sour. Sour. Yellow. Grape looking bulbs turning green and orange floating down the tributaries racing with the flow at a caterpillars drifting speed, bumping into and clinging onto logs and grasses while being consumed along the way by gray eyed fishes and jungle rodents falling victim from the lungs and collapsing into the anoxic bogs to become permanently preserved, an entombed time capsule in the making.

Maybe We should all (this of course looking at and thinking of things in a bit more of the longer cycle) just dive in with our circadian possessions to be a curiosity and window back in time to the next ice age which freezes up civilization in an albedo block of cold blue reflective preservation for the next alpha species to discover, scrutinize, and judge, immortalizing yourself beyond death into future epochs like a wooly mammoth or sabre tooth tiger in a tar pit. No, just a human with a lung full. Another Ice Man. Preserved. Brownish in a low oxygen, Anoxic, environment. Waiting like a dull glistening mummy cocooned in a sarcophagus to be unearthed for inspection by the investigators, or treasure seekers, curious of the past and looking for the answers that'll never be there. Leaving them only with speculations to please the pallet of the nagging thirst of infinite knowledge attempting to answer the age old questions dimwittedly perplexed over throughout time and all history of intellectual thought, like who are we and why are we here? And, oh yeah, along the way let me stab you in your weak scrawny little back so that I myself might proceed on more comfortably. Ultimately the strongest *shall* survive, in a catch 22, with the staunchest manufactured medicines to shun off the endless diseases that bombard a complex organism comprised of endless strings (which are separate life forms unto themselves), as well as the human species accepting of synthetic alterations for consumption and mutation.

Within two years, and only a few short seasons before the naturally occurring death of Grandpa Notts, and just a handful of weeks before the cancerous departure of Aunt Amanda, the uncontainable 3RS slowly cast out the mortal life selectively engineered and evolved into the moral fiber of Matt's mother, Danica, along with the countless other genetically programmed conscious souls that 3RS released from angst equaling any of the highest historical death counts produced by any other naturally occurring outbreak or epidemic, plague or disease, or even by the evil hand of man during any one of the numerous self-balancing exterminations recorded by either war or genocide.

Many people had convictions that 3RS was an answer to the not so perfect ways of man, a day of reckoning so to speak. There was even a belief by some that it was a retribution caused by disrespectful foreign climbers and their indiscriminate actions and lack of reverence for the sacred mountain 3RS first attacked. There came to be an unprecedented progressive movement, which picked up extremely enormous momentum as it marched forward, for a call out to all of mankind to conduct a global Day of Humiliation. There were actually three such of these Thursdays over a five month span that were universally acknowledged and observed as practiced Days of Humiliation. This was only possible at this time through the use of internet feed technology and was the first time a worldwide collectivity was successfully organized. It involved individual spiritual appeal, to the higher powers of personal preference, for all of the faithful, concerned, and anticipative participants to collectively will humanity to a better tomorrow free of 3RS via use of positive thought. It will never be able to be proven scientifically if this transcendence of spiritual belief was what actually led to the "divine disappearance" (as it was dubbed) of 3RS.

It was eventually found that certain people were actually resistant or unaffected by the 3RS disease and it was only through their stem-cell donations that the pandemic would be eradicated, consequently, in essence, mutating the human population through adaptive immunity. Infants and young children with maternal antibody protection were also found to be unsusceptible or immune. Resulting from the worldwide pooling of scientists researching and collectively attempting to eliminate 3RS, the CDC saw unprecedented advancements of new preventive medications as well as cures to long stubborn afflictions and infections. Then, all of a sudden, certainly faster than it manifested itself, 3RS ran its course and miraculously faded away, vanishing into near oblivion while ending its vexing scourge. The pestilent nuisance soon departed from the worried soul of humanity as the Golden Age of Medicine first opened up to the world to begin the continuous circularity of its perpetual tenure, which coincidentally advented itself at about the same time the comet Apophis was safely scurrying around its infamous gravitational keyhole, an event which highly reduced the risk of coming doom upon its next return.

Unfortunately for Matt's aunt Amanda her affliction and battle with breast cancer was prior to the immense unprecedented breakthroughs following the 3RS suppression. She did however much earlier, in the first decade of the new millennium, as a young adult receive the maiden and groundbreaking (yet controversial) three dose HPV vaccination which was mainly for the prevention of cervical cancer as well as for related vaginal and vulvar vexations, although initially not quite as effective on the latter two according to early studies. The first Gardasil injection during the introductory office visit and then the second six weeks later, with the final shot occurring six months after the first, all before she became active in her teen years. Sadly, white blood cell targeted vaccines, as well as HIV, breast cancer, and lymph node inoculations came into availability too late to be effective to prevent the aggressive breast cancer strain that expanded throughout her body and into her organs. The immunizations for breast cancer had been approved but just not quite on the market yet, plus these preventive injections needed to be given at a younger age to reap the full benefits. Aunt Amada would have needed to receive the boosters at the latest with her HPV shots, which down the road would progress into a single jab for multiple unwholesome disease preventions and leave a small birth mark looking scar similar to the polio blemish of the 1960's. Lamentably for the ill-fated lady, barely a third of the way through a fulfilled life, it would be almost a decade, from first prognosis, till the Golden Age of Medicine would perfect AEVB (Aggressive Engineered Virus Bombardment), spoken like a women's name and last initial, Ava B., which essentially dissolved and destroyed cancerous invasions into ones body.

Although not fool proof or 100% accurate, 3-D viewing of mammography illumination and later an ultrasound screening program on an annual basis were the best ways for breast cancer analysis before Genetic Disposition Scanning (GDS), even though these early tests were still after the fact revelations and assessments letting it be known (hopefully early) if the cancer is there, but not telling the poor victim it is coming beforehand. In Aunt Amanda's time early detection provided the best chance to overcome the cancer and live through the ordeal. Many women survived the harsh treatments and, with reconstructive surgery, were at least provided the small consolement of being augmented more endowed than before. The traditional chemotherapy Aunt Amanda had to endure left her bald, sullen, and haggard. Looking horrible at the funeral of Matt's mother, Danica, she barely had the strength to attend, but coinciding with the 3RS epidemic she in a way fit in as many individuals looked like, for lack of a better word, zombies; or perhaps just, "death worn over." Many people facing poor cancer odds of survival, or little to no chance of recovery from an extremely diminished way of life, opted for the pro-death choice of assisted suicide after it was passed into law, along with the acceptance of other numerous liberal laws that finally got recognized after decades of controversy.

Conversely Grandpa Notts did well to get by on his own right up to the end of his breeze swept, sun-shiny, colorfully highlighted days. Danica would stop in a couple of times a week to bring supplies or accompany the elderly trouper to the grocery store. Often the two would go out for a greasy breakfast at the "Yellow Diner," or for soup and sandwich if it was later in the morning and the old-timer didn't order his favorite, liver and onions. Grandpa Notts had a small terrier to keep him company and active but it seemed as the canine (Tuffy) quickly faded and aged so did the long lived veteran. After Danica fell ill, and eventually was overcome by 3RS, then Matt, when not already there to shovel snow or cut grass, became the one to regularly stop in the (to his generation gapped point of view) unpleasant and dusty old person and poor aim smelling house, even though it was really actually pretty well kept with a tandem of hard working cleaning ladies stopping in once a week to pick up, vacuum, mop, and scrub. Meals on Wheels also came over on a scheduled basis a few times a week to bring hot plates, which his doddering taste buds didn't particularly care for, but he tried not to be unappreciative of, as the time worn senior citizen enjoyed whatever crumb of human interaction fate might muster. The proud pensioner wanted to refuse the awful tasting dinners all together, but reckoned maybe he could choke them down and live with the (although friendly, to him they were meddlesome) officious humanitarians intruding a couple of times a week to dote on him. And he grew Forward to the routine of their arrival.

It was actually Matt who, later toward the familiar, found his great-grandfather close to the retiree's 103rd birthday and shortly after the social security office had just made one of their routine stops, which they do every so often to make sure that the person receiving their check is still alive and there isn't an unscrupulous relative continuing to cash in on the funds and not reporting the real recipient's death. They would mention to Grandpa Notts, during the well-being check, how incredibly fine he was doing and be amazed at his health, mobility, and longevity. The beyond golden yeared gentleman enjoyed having some company interested to hear about the antiquated story of his life and tales from WWII. In turn the Social Security Administration outreach crew, off the record, told the fixed income senior about some of their encounters, such as the near senile elderly widow they called Cat Lady, who was real to life living with eight cats and the only food in the cluttered house was the cupboards full of cans of cat food. The gray Grandpa Notts got a tickled defibrillation out of the relaying of this enfeebled behavior which later seemed only to be part of the build up to lighten him up for the final roadmap suggestion which he wasn't very accepting of. Graciously however, Grandpa Notts wasn't discovered by Matt in some type of feeble and dismal nursing home, that smelled of Clorox bleach and old people's ass, and his only reason to visit was out of guilt and to sneak in some M&M's because he felt sorry for him living in some type of mechanical hospital bed with band-aids from IVs on his arms and his jello and water setting out of his reach where the near invalid couldn't consume them without tracking down nursing assistance from somewhere within the undermanned facility, but would this guilt still be better than the inconvenience of taking care of on elderly relative in one's own home if that would have been the case?

One of the last times Grandpa Notts was able to actually get out and kick up his heels was at Matt and Amber's wedding celebration, after the pair finally decided to tie the knot. That is if shuffling out to stand next to the bride for a slow song or posing for a few holy pictures and family portraits would be considered strenuous activity, even though his steadfast and shatterproof ability to get around *was* quite impressive for a person of his unyielding age. Grandpa Notts did light yard work, such as weeding and pruning, as well as other home maintenance activities like the painting of fascia and trim boards on the outside of his sprawling ranch home, well into his nineties.

Least wise, without letting on with any complaining, Grandpa Notts didn't seem to suffer any physical ailments, health concerns, or other medical issues, even up to his final heart thumps. On a calm and tranquil November night not long after 3RS had evacuated our spherical plane, the tired patriarch passed on peacefully and quietly in his own bed without any pain (so it was assumed to lessen the concerned unknowingness of those grasping and remorsing his lonesome passing as no one was actually there at the side of the independent old man, to know if he *was* suffering or in pain, when he did finally take his last breath). Matt was later told by the coroner that it was probably two, maybe up to three days that Grandpa Notts laid, undiscovered curled up in the fetal position under the sheets, before Matt walked into his bedroom fighting off the bright morning sun filling the edge of the room, grimacing his eyes, and shining warm at the foot of the bed that fateful day he came over to check in on his squirrely and energetic next of kin. Grandpa Notts could have just been tired, and sick of all the loved ones precipitously passing on ahead of him, and just figured it was finally his time to give in and be with them and not go on living worrisomely wondering who would be the next to prematurely depart and encounter the snuffing out of their divine spark.

The previously self-possessed Matt was humbled to the last Notts standing. Now older, married, and more mellow, with a rightfully concerned anticipation of an inherited genetic mortality, he was these days consciously always a bit on edge wondering if his next breath may be his last following a long list of premature untimely fatalities. Grandfather, Will Jr., age fifty-two, Newport Crystalized lungs. Father, forty-one, cardiac arrest. Same aged aunt, Amanda, cancer. Middle aged mother, disease. Young adult son of father's friend, technological distraction. Grandmother Ruth Sanders and her husband Roy, sixties, carbon monoxide CO_2 inhalation, (which is ironic how an HVAC expert allowed himself and family to fall prey to air poisoning), and how, does the saying go about the shoe maker's children being the last to get a pair cobbled to their feet? The premature list could go on and on and also include several acquaintances sent away from this Earth, either by zealous acts of extremist terrorism or unforeseen natural disasters.

So Matt used his new found (finally inherited) wealth to check off the activities on his bucket list when not patiently acquiring more wealth, although he also must have inherited some of Grandpa Notts' valuable genes as the greatest of riches because it would be quite some time before he would succumb to deceasement. Using the mighty power of Silver Smith virtual currency he invested in his totally own vertical farming medical cultivation center. After agonizing and scrutinizingly getting the legal permits, following a charade of finger printing, back ground checks, and a general jumping through hoops, the affronted Matt went on to name his kick ass unworldly successful public corporation "Canned Abyss." He took advantage of this persuadable market and newly capitalized commodity, as they fired up a scant and sluggish economy equaling historic industrialized cotton and tobacco crop bail outs and catapulters. Between the lines cigarette companies were secretly supporting all manners of nicotine consumption and any and all styles of smoking behavior in order to promote the sales of their own products by any means possible, even though the addictive indulgences could practically sell themselves as a person missing out on their regular dose could tend to get a bit angry inside. This collaboration was because many of the people smoking marijuana also engaged in any number of the other numerous smoking fashions actively being practiced throughout this period.

After the passing of Grandpa Notts everything that was accumulated by all the relatives, over the many years, went to Matt. In the ancient attic of Grandpa Notts' home there was a treasure trove of family history. Countless old photos of Grandpa and Grandma Notts along with Will Jr. and Uncle Henry. Strange thoughts and emotions overcame Matt as he methodically rummaged through his heritage up in the allergen dusted loft built into in the rafters. Wondering about things like whatever happened to that shiny silver camping trailer, and why didn't he like the outdoors, fishing, and camping? Why hadn't he shown more respect towards those who preceded ahead of him; living, enduring, and flourishing to help mold his existence as it was at that exact moment across the linearity of time, and he conjured an infinite image that even a circle, if large enough, will have a line appear straight. All of these nagging raw emotions were turbulence inside of his meandering soul and stirred up more questions about the meaning and purpose of life for his racing mind to ponder.

Mixed in with some old time looking music records of unknown singing groups, and wedged between some old Western Union telegraphs, there was a 45 sized yellowed brown package saying, "BUY WAR BONDS AND STAMPS," in large red letters. It also said in the middle, in smaller blue capital letters, "play this record on any phonograph use new needle." On the bottom there was a small Davey Crockett looking fellow (with a musket held in one hand across the breast) stamped in like a miniature magazine cover. It read in varying sizes of capital lettering, "for victory buy United States war savings bonds stamps." Respectfully bordering the left and right of Pioneer Man in mid-sized red capitals was, "you help America" on one side and "you help yourself" on the other. That was presumably the back because there was a one and one half cent Martha Washington stamp on the other side (and a carrot nosed guy standing under a microphone which was as big as himself where he only reached the bottom of it, or just the top of its stand). Although obviously being the front with the address being there, it was folded up into this side making one think it should be the back. This side read, "Gem Blades bring you the recorded voice of- -". Gem Blades in red and this time underlined. Then the person who was recording their message for home filled in their name, the person to whom they were addressing (a large M was at the beginning to start the addressing), and the address, no zip code. So Your Sweetheart (presumably Grandpa Notts) recorded a message for **M**iss Margaret O'Leary, Flushing, New York. As Matt wondered what Grandpa Notts might have recorded from overseas to his future wife he realized that the events of the past shape the present and the only constant continually occurring is that things are in a perpetual state of change. Even way back then people wanted their far away loved ones to feel as if thousands of miles was only around the corner. Matt did manage to locate an old phonograph in the house, but the record was old and fragile, made of cardboard or something of such, and never was able to have its romantic message revealed again.

While each one of the timeline of family photos stirred sentiment in some manner or other, some of them stood out more than others. There was what seemed to be intended as a humorous photo of Uncle Henry fishing. It displayed a stringer of smaller sized fish while revealing the museful angler without his prosthetic arm. His joined functioning arm was outstretched conveying the message about the one that got away being as big as the length of one arm to infinity. There were also a couple of photos of the perfectly postured Grandpa Notts with his army buddies posing proudly over surrendered armaments stacked and piled as captured plunder, spoils destined for the ocean floor and smelting furnace. That was when Matt noticed out of the corner of his eye the handle, or Tsuka as he would later learn, of one of the easily recognizable as not being massed produced, Bizen forged work of art Japanese Samurai swords that Grandpa Notts brought back with him to the states. Hmm, this may take some investigation, he reflected to himself, but they sure would look pretty damn cool displayed on the wall in the man cave. The house, the Lincoln, a life insurance policy that the disciplined old man paid on regularly to the end, along with some stock certificates from IBM and Xerox. There was going to be more than enough extra wealth for him to inherit so maybe it would be good to just keep and display some of those priceless heirlooms of his family origins, such as the swords and Grandpa Notts' newly discovered dog tags (Will Jr.'s were set in his coffin with a pack of cigarettes and whatever pills were left in his medicine cabinet). Kind of like a little memorial corner with old photographs and trinkets displayed to honor those who came before. Matt could even take up the beer can collecting hobby and replace the collection of Uncle Henry's he had auctioned off years before, because now, after the epiphany of discovering his lineage, the rolled tin labels in a way were missed. The reborn Matt would make the new assemblage a display which would be even bigger and better.

There were plenty of hobbies and activities to keep the energetic Matt Notts fully occupied as his financial and business investments, inheritance, and Amber's thriving oral beautification clinics, were doing lifetimes of earnings a year at a time. Donations were a full time occupation to dutifully keep tax expenses to a minimum and this family desired to achieve the ultimate American dream, to reach tax freedom day on January 2nd. Environmental causes were a favorite Notts sponsorship. Project Nanook, for example, was involved with the corralling of endangered wildlife into an immense sanctuary to protect the Earth's natural species from loss of habitat, poaching, and ultimately extinction. Within the boundaries of these highly protected game reserves many distressed and suffering species made a strong and thriving recovery. Reaching National landmark status this was one of the huge success projects of 21st century awareness and assertiveness.

Economic delineated acronymic government agencies frequently spring into existence throughout history to aid, inform, protect, regulate, and control society and citizens, or the environment: SSA, FDA, CDC, FBI, DEA, ATF, INS, IRS, NOAA, ERB, EPA, and on and on. There was a rushing stream of newly formed administrative organizations to attempt to counter act the ever demanding ecological needs, and stifle public fear and strife, as the voting public's beseeching outcries of concern became noticed. Even though the anxiety distressed populace's genetically inherited consumptive actions went in the opposite direction towards the other end of the spectrum, further showing the need for a government to hold society's hand like a school child crossing a loud and busy intersection.

Yet still in charge of overseeing all of the numerous little spinoff agencies popping up, The EPA was ever evolving into appendages of nothing more than censored monetarily forgiven and expunged programs that were maintained cleansed, backed and corroborated with efforts validating and encouraging a warranted bowdlerized blue pencil advocate of championed research and development assisted by pardoned subsidies justified by sponsoring humanitarian aid and assistance for the well-being of mankind.

As the 21st century was rolling on ever closer to its midway point, and in relatively prompt response to the eye opening events that unfolded after awakening from 3RS, The Environmental Recovery Act (ERA) was passed explicably justifiably hand in hand with The Environmental Recovery Tax (ERT). With a loan of government funds to be repaid by the tax, The Environmental Recovery Bureau (ERB) was formed to oversee the use of the astronomical resources allocated, and to make sure that they would actually make it to their purpose of bandaging up the planet. A previously introduced Carbon Footprint Tax (CFT) was already in the negative from the extensive infrastructure and municipal projects it siphoned down to, like the person winning the lottery to be broke in five years. Some five year plan. But this new determined resolution was a necessity decisive to proceeding to the future. Surviving with a vision of a better tomorrow the techno-native Millennials were thinking differently than the previous generation of greed drawn and driven baby boomers. **They** could see where the path the prior tenants' selfish free will reign was leading and how it has left their inherited biological realm.

This generation of cultivators of the natal domain had the dubious distinction of being dubbed as lazy, but in defense they preferred to use their minds and intellect to create solutions and come up with better ways to advance mankind, and rejuvenate the ailing planet with fresh approaches to extract and manipulate the Earth's natural resources while not further breaking down its delicate cycle and balanced equilibrium.

The first and foremost concern was to reduce carbon in the air. The large scale endeavor called Project Lungwort, PL with its air "pills" or diamond "pills," was first initially undertook around this time, ironically coinciding closely with man first setting foot on its atmosphere free neighboring planet. Equipped with two 75 Volt seventh generation lithium ion phosphate batteries possessing internal positive temperature coefficient current limitation, and a small solar collection panel which would keep the battery at the lowest level charging while the piston like action of the control mechanism would be producing a continuous recharging effect, even throughout a calm night, as each individual pill unit would stay in motion springing up and down using the near continual movement of the ocean waves to act similar to a tire pump in tandem with the tens of thousands of other Lungwort "pills." Interpreted as an acronymic play from reading out P L, (and from high above they actually looked similar to miniature floating aspirin), the pills bobbing in the ocean where bunched alongside of each other strategically tethered securely to the high pressure synthetic diamond farm regularly receiving the carbon far below the brightly lit surface.

The proceeds from the production of the perfectly octated cultivated underwater diamonds (CUDs) was used to offset the enormous cost to construct and maintain the domineering and dynamic carbon clean-up projects being vigorously attempted, but why not use the by-products for capitalistic gains. Generally Capitalism will croon the public anyway. Once its harmful dirt is no longer able to be ignored then there is a small insulting attempt of compensation, like eat this tasty candy till your teeth fall out, and afterwards, "here have some applesauce coupons." It was the same monotone voice echoing in your head, "If you, your child, a loved one, a friend, or anyone you have had an association with, has suffered or experienced ill-effects such as an injury or disorder, lack of function, medical ailments, inability to socially interact, mental impairment, death, or otherwise loss of life quality due to exposure, use, or consumption of said prescription, device, chemical, product, suggestion, whatever." Then contact the firm at no charge and get in line for *your* twelve dollar entitlement out of the twenty-five million dollar award of financial restitution. No worry of compensation neurosis here. The spirit of group class-action is like government attempting to push the tax burden onto the wealthy which just never will manifest more than as a well-intended theory, suggestion, or proposal. From a historical standpoint a true economic golden age for mankind can never occur. The small percent in control, of the soul of whatever wealth status system is being distributed and practiced, inherently prohibit and block the lesser off percent from becoming equal to them. The congregations of commoners are being given just enough to keep them believing they're graciously fulfilled, and not from rebelling, while those who are above are simultaneously offering up some type of religion to give complacent hope.

Project Lungwort and the introduction of its highly demanded 21st century commodity and resource of cultured diamonds coupled with its stock going public, simply coincided with the history of trade. Although it would be quite some time before the shares would see those significant dividends, the venture capitalists like Matt Notts who got aboard early were well compensated for their long term patience and support, while partnering with the government still maintained a strong and honorable patriotic endorsement to buoy the nationalistic programs championing activism for all proud citizens to revere as the worldwide platform perceived a distinctive image inducing reverence and respect during this leg of history's advancing voyage.

On the land ISHMAEL (International Safety and Humane Management Agency for Earth Life) oversaw the Inky Caps which were the forefathers of artificial cyber-integrated singularity forests (ACISF, or AC forests). The first prototype Inky Caps with their mainly mechanical make-up were more machine like, making them further susceptible to malfunction and not nearly as self-sustaining and reliable as the later AC forests which were alive of a life-form as man could blend and create out of high-tech nuts and bolts. Isn't the basic miniature make-up of nature when broken down to the smallest individual blocks only just an assemblage of simple organic nano machines anyway? The Inky Caps got their name from their tar like resin, which was a residue bubbling on top of them causing the carbon machines to look like some enormous type of sticky mushroom. Their rows of fabricated foundations were precisely plotted to collect the atmospheric carbon into the carbon ranch silos placed alongside power plants coupled with plastics factories to produce eco-friendly polymerized products on a large scale industriousness. These new age plastics were designed to break down and be biodegradable at a rate which was enormously more efficient and acceptable than the earlier archaic 1900's traditional plastic engineering allowed.

Late 20th century slogans such as simply saying "Go Green" and "Save the Planet," as well as the putting out of any of the other such catchphrases and advertisements saying "Earth Friendly," just wasn't going to be enough. Much of this was just a ploy to get people to buy more merchandise and new products. If the companies could make the consumers believe that their purchase was making a difference to the environment then they have got a sale with repeats to follow. Buy this product it's "Green," it's "Recycled." It's new and improved, "safer and cleaner," "Eco-Conscious," but in reality maybe only better than a much older substandard product put out scores of years previous, and yet most likely still only meeting minimal regulated requirements. It was clear that the consumers were not the ones that were going to make the difference. They just buy and trash things at too high of a rate. The key, for the most ill-disposed and ignorant abuser and even those who were actually unaware of their multitude of misbehaviors toward mother Earth, lied in the ecologically aware concepts and breakthroughs refining the philosophies and principles, as well as the outcome, of environmental co-existence to effect humanity's perception and attitude.

ISHMAEL was in charge of cleaning up polluted areas and waterways. They set out to keep more areas unspoiled by man with natural conserves set aside with limited permitted access, such as in their apex capstone Nanook National Park. This was done in more of a traditional fashion and put jobless individuals to work, but not making them look like jail road crews in orange jumpsuits reading "DOC" on back. Environmental awareness programs pushed unemployment down to an all-time low rate with huge tax break incentives, as well as housing service benefits and grants, offered to those working in the environmental industry. There was a reward or bounty on the books, of one half the proceeds of the hefty fine for polluting, to anyone turning in an offender. Littering was taken very seriously with strict enforcement of environmental code violations and harsh penalties such as a three strike statute. Anyone committed of three environmental crimes of misuse would have to serve a five year sentence. Everyone realized that they were an inhabiting and contributing component of the sensitive and friable Mother Planet and thus an environmental pride was created with most all people adhering to an acute awareness of the delicateness of nature and, along with the introduction of eco-co-existent packaging, humanity would eventually subdue new land pollution significantly.

The 22nd century's Environmental Singularity occurred through the 21st century taking the first baby steps toward a sustainable Mother Earth coexisting with the needs of overflowing human populations, as well as fundamental development of practical scientific advancements like the Inky Cap, IP, "pills," Green and Biodegradable Carbons, practical application of high efficiency renewable energy sources, and also other revolutionary new types of manufactured waste friendly packagings that could, in a relatively short amount of time, "vanish" into thin air or break down into basic hydrogen and oxygen. The sincere dedication (brought about by a jump out of this burning building or die attitude) to bio-reclamation undertakings was key to the next decades being cleaner than the previous ones, as well as the upcoming centuries being cleaner than the prior few.

Too bad fixing environmental disregard wasn't as simple as the everyday task of loading domestic trash and waste into a large container and catapulting it out into the dark frigid interplanetary vacuum, strung together by the mass of its highly mysterious and elusive anti-elasticity matter, (AEM, formerly referred to as dark matter), from the platform of a space elevator, towards the sun, or Jupiter, to incinerate the rubbish. Once the realization that everyone was interwoven in the Mother Land together occurred, then each individual would intuitively play their unassuming role of meekness as the mind would become the overall link of all in one and one in all, and the change in human nature could occur. This actually led to people being less wasteful and using only what they truly needed. There would be no more boundaries of mind and will, as inherent righteousness is a collective of each owns will. As the will of one and the will of all come together to make the will of one, there is no reason to have a will other than the will of all. He who is not bonded to the will of all is freezing in the cold, desolate, separate, alone.

These concepts of one and all linked were only enforced by the mainstream scientific view of life switching over its thought to encompass a more true examination observing the meaning of life and what is moving around in the universe to eventually build up to the apex life forms strung together by countless miniscule ones interacting together on a clockwork like molecular scale. The smaller we magnify the view to focus in on things the more activity and movement we see to the smallest particle being a life form containing a life energy of its own classification. If you can squeeze water out of a rock then isn't the rock alive? It is the basic elements themselves that contain the life. Since the elements that build the universes and life are everywhere then life is everywhere because it is in the substance surrounding everything. And all of this leads to the greatest ambiguity concerning the big bang and the nature of the infinite universe. If it is infinite how can it be growing and moving away, or outward, because infinity encompasses everything including that which is beyond, even though matter can not be created or destroyed? If it can not be created or destroyed it must, both, be there and it must be alive. So matter is life and maybe from our momentary perspective the universe is moving away only because it is flowing cyclic, circling like a galaxy, encompassing infinity and all of its matter and anti-elasticity matter. Maybe just reverbing like an accordion or bouncing like a dribbling basketball in slow motion, spinning around a central force the same as most objects in our perspective, but the perspective is just too enormous, and the speed unnoticeably changing to perceive, as if we, as a speck of dust upon the solar system, still might only be observing the world as flat.

A short time before the end of the infancy stages of Environmental co-existence, and about the time the Pyramid of King Ay was unearthing itself from the sifted dessert sands of Saqqara (which still was a bit of a way to half way to the morning that the 22nd century would dawn), Amber decided she wanted to use her (quickly fading) new and fresh position of newlywed marriage status, to raise a child with Matt before it would be too late. Due to the fact she had unconsciously blinked past her fortieth birthday, from being so busy with their full-time hectic careers and the everyday feverish consumption of time, the couple was understandably having some biological trouble conceiving. The only choice they had to realistically create a birth inside the yearning womb of the eager and ripened Amber was going to involve some scientific assistance. Realizing this fact the married couple went to The Cosmopolitan Fertility Clinic where, as it was guaranteed to succeed within or a full return of funds, on the third assertive in vitro attempt, after a numerous series of heart wrenching disappointments, she was finally going to bear a child, a son, and thus the Notts lineage would continue forward.

Landon Jeremiah Notts was born on February 28th a little over four years after the death of Grandpa Notts. LJ was going to be perfect and flawless in every way. The ideal child that a couple could want nothing more of. With embryo screening and pre implantation genetic diagnosis there was almost no risk of any DNA defects, genetic flaws, or even the slightest chance of any genetic pollution. Fortunately of course there was also not even the remotest possibility of fetal alcohol syndrome (like Will Jr. should of had to fear with the conception of LJ's grandfather Jeremiah). The pampered watchful upbringing would involve only the most exceptional ambiances the facilitating world had to offer. A modern day human to one day become the standard, customary, and compliant communal component of the mundane turn into the 22nd century (in his own individual way of course) as a contributing caretaker of the evolution of human progression towards its inevitable course of complete biological fulfillness.

Home schooled on Chippewa Computer Classroom LJ and the other kids didn't befriend playmates in typical fashion. With the Virtual Interactive Classroom (VIC) the progressive Chippewa School brought the learning to the child and not the student to the school. This became the standard method to educate. The phrase "home school" took on a different course of meaning than one thinking of some type of Puritan Family educating their twelve children, in their historically landmarked kitchen, to instill their rhetorical traditional beliefs fed in with the three R's. LJ who was better off than all but a small few had a complete and all-inclusive classroom of his own right inside the Notts' expansive Frank Lloyd Wright inspired contemporary estate sprawling over their gorgeous and generous, water stream edged, wooded home acreage.

With an Internet Feed in the home all the children could link and school together, whether or not they had a nanny, play room, Chef's Choice Smart Waiter, or an IP. The Internet Feed (IF), was the basic preliminary joint mapping sensor headset that allowed an individual to navigate their computers and devices truly hands free (yet with some dangling cranium connection wires) through tele-operation (or thought).....as what IF. Energy Frequency Vibration (EFV) technology allowed the alpha frequency meditation waves to admit children virtual entrance and attendance allowing them to become able to see the images as if they were physically sitting at their hard and uncomfortable, plastic and wooden, desks in a material classroom. It was the same type of cap white collars used to conduct business and read the news as housewives did their gossip. Although quite amazing in itself the IF didn't last very long. By the time LJ was ready to "attend" school most of the children being raised and reared with the 7G technology during the infancy of the Golden Age of Medicine had an IP (Implant Phone) injected into their cerebral fluid, similar to medical neural dust, and the annoying "skull caps" became a thing of the past like all other technological stepping stones such as the 8-track cassette, video cassette recorder, and cassette tape answering machines.

As with most progressive parents of this time Matt and Amber encouraged the arts and crafts equal to mathematics and science. They believed if the children were to find their true way in adulthood it was important to nurture their creative side of discovery at an early age. In Amber's house other Chippewa school children were allowed, and encouraged, to come over to interact and participate alongside LJ.

When first being announced to the public it was considered unveiling, the ingenious touchless implant technology replacing the Internet Feed, designated as an ID (Implant Device), but early marketing acceptability studies discovered this preliminary name sounded too Big Brother. How do you advertise that everybody must now have an ID? It made it sound like you were being carded for cigarettes or alcohol, and the implant was tracking you and your thoughts while controlling you, instead of the actual reality of the matter which really was that you are controlling it to control whatever it is you have desired it to be synced with. Although not a phone in the traditional sense, phone was a more comfortable universal term in which everyone could relate to and accept.

The IP involved a simple matter of using one's own thought to go where one wished to be guided in the sphere of accessible information. It put your "phone" into your thoughts to communicate with others instantaneously, truly hands free, and really hands off, without wearing the slightly cumbersome Internet Feed Cap. The haptic display visualized in the user's mind could control whatever the IP was linked to. This was only the tip of its basic functioning as a BMI (Brain Machine Interface). Eventually in time there *were* drawbacks to be discovered and circuits to be tweaked as the face of human existence evolved.

In reality technology such as the IP evolved out of the necessity for ease of use, by improving quality and function to lessen the detrimental complications and downfalls one could experience by becoming distracted from other activities while manipulating a device, such as texting and driving, or tuning and whatever other physical activity one is engaged in. This was real progress. For starters the continual loss of worker production since the advent of the smart phone was finally being stemmed. When initially introduced into culture the status quo trembled and this new age instrument of telephone evolution was considered (perhaps somewhat skeptically) to be a breakthrough truly beneficial to mankind and not simply just another technology created to exploit the natural resources of an ever weakening planet which was only just in the infancy stages of beginning Environmental Co-existence. The IP would go on to be considered an invention to become a universal necessity, a true clean progress that would become a helpful benevolence to the evolution of humanity, and this in more ways than just from a technological standpoint.

Besides the zealous military operation applications which drive and dominate the advancement of most new technologies forward, it was actually the humanitarian necessity of creating realistically functioning robotics for amputees that progressed the development of BMI to the point of the IP. It was too bad that Uncle Henry wasn't alive during this innovative time to see and use these cutting edge advancements which would make him feel as if he actually had his real arm reattached and not just sensing some ghost tinglings from his lost appendage.

The Internet Feed and IP were first designed for better information communication to replace traditional portable phone and data technology while also allowing for enhanced fundamental linkage to control synced mechanical devices. It is likely when automobiles were introduced nobody foresaw drunk driving deaths and carjacking. Likewise all repercussions from Implant Phone injection haven't yet come full circle, as new related industries and different useful functions continually pop-up overnight. A whole new clinical medical industry arose from different conditions directly related to this evolution of man and technology. As the first generations were being born into the Implant Phone Era, it was hard to calculate the full scope of Speech Utilization Detriment Syndrome (SUDS), where humans are communicating primarily through thought and not applying traditional speech pallet muscles and brain waves creating diminished speech motor skills and a lacking ability to speak. The more concerning issues were unless the IP is put into a sleep mode the brain can't click off and isn't being allowed the required night's rest needed for recharging, so a whole new area of sleep deprivation is opened up. Going hand in hand the device has features so highly addictive it makes 1950's zombie-like families staring into a fuzzy-lined television screen seem normal and productive.

The Electronic Shaman and Resonance Drum (ES and RD, respectfully) were Upps, or Uploads, that could for extra monthly fees enhance the use of the cartelized IP device to a virtual state to access the gift of higher awareness and thought. Most all exquisite artistic creations of the late 21st century were masterfully accomplished through the use of such Upps as these, or similar ones like Muse Genie and Purple River. These strongly powerful awareness Upps tapping into the etheric plane were programmed only for allowable use, connection, and access in specific locations obeying strict regulations for a safely controlled environment to monitor the distraction of a near loss of physical consciousness in the material world. This was so that no injury would befall the participants engaging the practice of a universal mind and thought awakening encompassing the encircling perception of their complete inner soul awareness, or cause any threat, danger, or harm to others nearby either. There was some residual dilatation and loss of time cognition experienced from the electro-access synchrony of the chemical brain, thus it was important to be careful when physically switching out of an Upp mode. As well there also could be some overwriting lingering memories to mentally contend with over the upcoming hours. Behind the scenes in reality the most advanced and far reaching IP Upps, like Intuition Arousal, were strictly regulated or even just simply kept out of commercial public access altogether.

Almost like wisdom coming in ones dreams through an out of body like experience such humanitarianly helpful and nudging Upps as The Translucent Soul and White Light intensified reality awareness spiritually allowing an extra sensory collective recognition interface. It was preached by the artisans of the day to bend your destiny, willing it through your artistic visions. It was unclear if the IP and its mind altering spiritually awakening awareness Upps truly conjured and created divine interventions and inspired genius, or if there could even still actually be a true "aha" moment of epiphany and realization.

One thing for certain is that if an outsider was looking in from an earlier time period they would have at first had a hard time understanding the idyllic symphonic contentment of the meshed individuals happily paired, and harmoniously interconnected with their perfect "soul mate," through the widespread use of Implant Phone enhancement. To those theoretical outsiders looking in, this world would have made for creepy scenes of a peaceful universal unity socially overflowing almost filthily. Were humans really meant to be so content, cohesive, and blissful with such a unified peaceful and unselfish connected co-existence towards each other and their planet? A so perfect world seems to put things out of balance creating an impending sense of putative doom. Was this the true destined intent of the gift of critical making, or just the inevitable outcome and by-product?

The IP was the very same "technology" that would in less than a couple of years be helpful to allow the breakthrough needed for the operation and eventual production of the first consumer based LLV (Lenticular Levitation Vehicle). Times had changed. Human controlled vehicles were quite a rare sight at this time anyhow, as fully autonomous vehicles were king of the road. The mainly older-aged throwback old-school individuals who did want to engage in the frivolous activity, where the illogical ritual was still legally allowed, generally had diminished driving skills and were poor operators out of practice. It may be remembered like the riding of a bicycle, but nobody wants to fall off or wipeout due to lack of habitual repetition.

The IP, the LLV, they go hand in hand. It is sort of ironic how certain breakthroughs come about near simultaneously, yet it could never be discovered if such things are pure coincidence or if there is a silent celestial hand guiding the way. It seems everything is just already there to be inevitably discovered. Waiting for us to reach with our Implant Phones or our LLVs. The Akashic hall of records, the cosmic well of knowledge, readily accessible. Floating out there, like the IP in our brain fluid, for all to read using the luminiferous spirituality of the Implant Phone circumnavigating the world wide river of the "internet" web, or the universal zero point field. Everyone understanding a little differently the things understandably different to understand. That is how the LLV came to be.

The LLV wasn't wholly new technology. It was pretty much just generally common and available technologies that were already out there, but just needed to be arranged differently. The two Varnett brothers, identical twins Lance and Lane, were, from a young age, endlessly tinkering mysteriously and secretively in their sheds, garages, and pole barn; with drones, magnetic devices repelling each other, liquid metals such as mercury, translucent solids, autonomous self-driving and aviation navigation systems, 3D replicated fiber-reinforced thermoplastics, smart glues, and endless other various types of electronics and scientifically specialized appliances and gadgets....all linked with an Internet Feed. It's easy to get the picture. Their workshop was a hodgepodge. Like going to the natural history museum and seeing one of those extinct, unbelievably freakish, hybrid-looking creatures conjoining familiar characteristics of two commonly recognizable, but completely different, living animals that someone haplessly fused together. Even so it would only be less than a couple of short years beyond its introduction that the IP, with its practical multimodal tactical feedback, would overcome the tele-impedances and become the key final piece to Lance and Lane's LLV puzzle.

The average grade-schooler knows that magnetism can attract or repel, and this was the theory that the Varnett brothers utilized and applied to have their levitation vehicle be navigated, by whichever firmament it chose to swim and pass through. It was a simple matter of programming the QGA to automatically adjust when harnessing and manipulating the push and pull effects of the giant Earth magnet that we all live on. Don't be mistaken these mechanically inclined siblings weren't mere mechanics or auto technicians, they were physicists and scientists gifted with being able to visualize the inner workings, outcome, and end product of intricate electronic and mechanical devices in which they could make up, invent, and blueprint in their heads on a Tesla like plane.

An accelerometer and a magnetic field disrupter were generated by the pyramid shaped superactinide Quartz-Gyro Accelerator (QGA, in which the Varnetts wisely patented) allowing the rotational inertia, of electromagnetic oscillations manipulating zero point fluctuation, to create a vacuum, through the utilization of the Casimir effect, which propelled (or repelled and pulled to be more descriptive) the LLV precisely and safely to where desired. With the advanced and innovative developments in practical production procedures of hybrid orbital transition metals, the neo-liberation elements were becoming ever more abundant, rocketing the flying car to actuality. Couple that with the fact that one shuttle load of Helium 3 collected from a quiet, empty, atmosphere free uninhabited celestial body would provide U.S. energy needs for over fifty years, the inevitable reality that fossil fuels would finally have to be let go, after almost two centuries of gluttonous consumption, was hard for some of the hardliners of its related fields of industry to accept. That is why the ink company needs to diversify into digital data storage and the microbial paper mill needs to have a wing producing e-readers.

A person thinks of a flying car (LLV) and they think of a UFO or the Avro-car, but this wasn't the case. It mainly could operate the same as any other normal autonomous vehicle out there on the roads. It was programmed, or chipped, not to enter the strictly enforced no fly zone restrictions around densely populated urban areas, where it *could* forever stay solely operated as a land vehicle if so desired. The LLV would come to have an altitude ceiling of 12,000 feet in the open fly zone areas. This was far above the 500 foot private and municipal drone level yet still well below military air space and the normal pressurized cruising patterns of the doomed commercial flight elevations which for another generation or so hung onto some bygone romanticism about it, similar to what riding rails across country in a passenger train might invoke. Each LLV was connected to all with a link chip, the same as the self-driving piloted autos on the land, assuring no unwanted collisions, near misses, or crashes. That brings up a subject which is something that always seemed to be amazing and unbelievable. If someone could build a "UFO" to travel through space, or time, or whatever, while being nearly undetectable, how could they not build one not to crash? Say in New Mexico for example?

In the 1950's and 1960's there was a German micro car built by an after the war defunct military plane manufacturing company. The best and most knowledgeable aviation experts of course got clipped over to the United States and Soviet Union. Some of those who were left in Germany went into the auto industry and produced some of the finest, ingenuitive, and most reliable human controlled vehicles of the time. One car that was engineered and didn't quite meet those benchmarks was a small goofy looking 3-wheeled bubble car called the Messerschmitt. It was an early urban subcompact prototype, perhaps a little ahead of its time (all it needed was an electric motor). With its in-line seating and opening up over the top canopy it resembled more of an airplane than a land vehicle. That's why it (or maybe also the 60's space race inspired Pinin Farina X Sedan) is a good comparison to the Varnett Geeks' LLV, which did in a remote way resemble a double front ended Messerschmitt, but on a slightly larger 2 or 3 to one scale. Both were innovative. One was ahead of its time and the other was long awaited in consumer imagination, finally coming into fruition a hundred years or so after first envisioned by a future looking populace.

After overcoming the FAA and DOT hybridization the LLV was still like any normal car with electric motors kept in the wheels for road use. Two wheels powering the land travel while the other two wheels are re-charging themselves while spinning. To function properly in flight the QGA had to be positioned in the center of the LLV. The seating was one in front, one in the back, and one along each side, totaling four, sort of in a diamond pattern around the securely contained QGA. The LLV was also equipped with substantial compartment space alongside the smooth edges of the outer rim for ample cargo storage.

To explain its operation and power production in somewhat simple terms imagine pouring water along the edge of a cylindrical pitcher to produce a spinning cyclone effect as it is filling up. This tub drain like circulation motion is what will ultimately create the magnetic field. A superactinide hybrid orbital transition metal (shot-m), generally Unhexquadium, is "poured" into the quartz lined cylinder, or the patented QGA, continuously recycling itself back in, pumping around the edges, spinning ever faster and building up more and more momentum, until a magnetic field is generated and oscillates around the outer shell of the LLV. The LLV itself was comprised of a lightweight titanium alloy frame with a memory Teflon membrane precisely coated with a glazed ceramic bio-paint DC sputter coated to create a type of terahertz plasmonic skin. Since the magnetic field was oscillating out from the center and around to encompass the exterior casing of the LLV, the inside was in a type of bubble and unaffected by outside or atmospheric conditions. The occupants within the vehicle were thus being protected from external forces, sort of like being inside the epicenter of a blast or earthquake. The eye of a tornado, or the event horizon of a black hole. Applying the Lorentz Force laws of physics it was only needed to use ones IP to activate the NOLO switch and communicate a desired destination. Eventually the vehicles would become mainly communal and used in rotation programs with an ant or insect like linkage of tasking which knew the daily commuting habits of its riders.

Later in its maturation the LLV would Copy another page out of nature's eons of perfecting, just like all great breakthroughs seem to mimic in some way or another. The final sputter coated outside layer was also a bio-skin incorporating attributes of the chameleon and the bat. The cloaking wasn't for any secrecy but to produce a calming effect for passengers darting around in the skies unaware of the bumper to bumper proximity of the other LLVs around them. One didn't need to travel for necessity as if they were being exhilarated at an amusement park. Part animal and part machine the electrically charged bio-skin also grew tiny hair follicles. These were sensors cross engineered from those of the bat to aid the navigation as a bat can fly "blind" at night by using its tiny hairs to make minute split second maneuvers. This assisted the bee and ant like inspired networking chipped into the complex system linking all LLVs together to completely guarantee collision free travel.

Before the height of all this technology befalling mankind, LJ went to a school with the other children. The school building itself was actually only attended two times a week for physical education and social interaction augmentation. Half the students would attend for two days while the other half were participating with them through the Interactive Classroom Interface (ICI). The following next two days the students would alternate and the fifth day, Friday, all student's classes were held through the Interactive Classroom Interface. It was the same as the United States Postal Service cutting delivery days to save government money. The office hours and delivery schedule only needed human employees Monday and Tuesday, and then again on Friday and half the day on Saturday. For the school children a physical touchable attendance which gathered the yearning, inquisitive, and thirsting for knowledge youth of the day, was essential for the maturing students to create the real life group interactions needed for building developmental social skills. An attribute and appreciation which could only genuinely be formed within the tangible surroundings of a concrete material place such as a school.

One day LJ's best friend Asher came over to his house after school let out. When they arrived and took off their Zoot brand jackets in the foyer, the favorite meals they craved appeared inside the food dispenser at the head of the long massive wooden dining room table emblazed with the bright afternoon sun. The unphased LJ expected his whims to be there when he walked in the door, but Asher, who wasn't brought up as well off as LJ and never had experienced a data thought machine, was a bit amazed to say the least. Although Asher had heard of them, the young perplexed curiositor never actually first hand witnessed or encountered a data thought machine, or DTM. He wasn't really quite sure deep down if he could reasonably believe with complete certainty that such farfetched hybrid technological appliances did in fact exist. Seeing and experiencing it for the first time was love at first sight. There it was before he even thought about what it was that he wanted to swallow. The refreshment and food that he desired was whipped up instantaneously and then spit out between the glimmering holographic logo of the Chef's Choice Smart Waiter, Chef's Choice being the manufacturer's name. Asher momentarily forgot that implant phones are hypothetically never truly off for traditional fundamental human interaction. Supposedly all of this inner argon thule minded anticipation was made possible just through a connection generated and sent out by his Implant Phone tracking his lifestyle and daily patterns.

Another day, a little later into adolescence, when the new technology was swallowing up the old like the waves of an ocean and changing the world at an unprecedented pace, the spirited boys were vigorously rough housing down in LJ's recroom. An ancient Greek marble statuette setting on top of the guilded and ornate wooden fireplace surround was accidently lightly brushed against by the distinctive blade wave of one of Grandpa Notts' relinquished Bizen masterpieces, thus causing the ancient Greek carving to teeter and eventually fall over. After time pausingly crashing down in a flash of memory, and shattering into shards of pieces, no amount of new and improved Super Smart Glue was going to fix this explosion. LJ and his to become life-long companion Asher had a secret they needed to cover up. To hell with the Hellenistic head that lie broken on the floor. They could just go to the sintering station of the tool room, down load some specs from known images for prototyping a digital model, and then use one of the Notts home's 3-D laser replicating systems to perform an attempt at spraying off a new falsely fabricated version. Unless examined under extreme scrutiny no one would notice any difference in the modularity of the new piece. The new sculpture would cure and could be removed from the pillar dock in a few hours. The reality was they simply shouldn't have been handling those priceless antique swords.

A lesson in mortality is absorbed as youths *may* be so exceptionally quick and smart, hitting their device buttons on the head so sharp and accurately, but even so this time those two messed up by irresponsibly and erratically playing with those lethal Samurai swords. The hand may be quicker than the eye, but the eye still is no match for the quickness of the mind, which in turn is really no match for the quickness of the data thought machines (such as a Smart Waiter) which when observed in the slowest of motion is actually processing and happening before it actually does occur in our known reality. Who though really needs to think when what is desired shows up on the doorstep seconds before you actually thought you needed it, or wanted it, or when you reach into your Smart Waiter food dispenser and what you have a taste for is there before you actually craved it. So why do we even need to think at all? Use of independent thought has been replaced by the necessity of thought machines which do the thinking for us more efficiently, and ergonomically so to speak. Eventually time slipped past the sculpted marble Greek bust occurrence with no harm no foul, and none the wiser of a cover-up. LJ later would just chalk up the incident as a spent advance of family inheritance.

LJ's parents Matt and Amber invested seriously and smartly in what they considered to be the perfect investments, the Varnett's LLV and stock in VWC, Vision Wirefree Communication, which was the primary preliminary IP provider. They didn't really need the extra assets. It was just the way the cards played out. The Notts family portfolio was well diversified from medicine to metallurgy. Even though a wealthy or well educated person's aire may unwittingly convey an unaware condescending type of obtuseness expressing arrogance and snobbery, this was not the case with Matt and Amber. Sincere meekness and modesty was true of their disposition even before it was realized that with the IP every class can be even to the same things in spirit and thought; with equal knowledge and awareness. A confident person might look to a less gifted or less fortunate Micawber type individual for worldly advice, if the two are like-minded and similar in ideals and views, via envision remembrance.

As LJ grew older, and developed intellectually, the IP inadvertently created a noticeable inequality of intelligence and consciousness. The IP expounded his inherited spiritually analytical remote viewing intellect which questioned the human existence and role. His visualization of colors, tastes, sounds, and smells left impressions of time's all-encompassing presence, which is always there, always ahead and always past, in some type of cosmic Mount Meru providing all knowledge. He built on the righteously pondering presumptions of his genetic ancestry, such as those irony based collective ramblings of Uncle Henry, Grandpa Notts, and sometimes even his naturally selected grandfather, Jeremiah.

LJ enjoyed to ruminate and reason alongside the factions supporting a calculated mass of the finite number of the universe, no matter how astronomical it may be. These arguments and debates would start off by taking the linearity of the number three. The basic never ending fraction one into three, .33 for infinity. The number, a number, any number, is a representation to count specific units. Although the number may be infinitely fractioned and go on forever, it needs to be at a lineal point to continue from, either forwards or backwards. So although a number fraction, or the universe, may be infinite, it is at a point of expansion at this very moment with a finite number counted to its present state, being the point it is at right now, and then countably continuing on indefinitely. It is only needed to have larger symbols of numeric expression to represent the numbers we cannot fathom. If the universe is expanding it is at a precise finite point of expansion right now, or else it could not continue on forever. There absolutely is a number to count the point the universe is at at this exact moment.

It is like saying the grains of sands in the seas are infinite because we don't have the capability to count or grasp the number, yet they are only the numerically finite sands of our Earth and its calculated mass, and no matter how large the number may be to count them, it is a number counting the matter which is physically there, now at this point of flow, with a mass that theoretically can be calculated. Just because a number may still be counting at this point of time doesn't mean the number is infinite even though it may go on infinitely. This demonstrates how the words infinite or infinity should not be used loosely for their true integral composition is a concept human intellect will never be able to completely comprehend, even though the concept itself and its use as a number equivalent may be necessary to form advanced mathematical calculations and equations.

As the future becomes the past, in its own meandering straightforward linear fashion, it seems that all of what has occurred was purposefully set into place to properly bring things to where they are in the present. This makes the events that transpire pre-determined as they cause these proceedings to take place for a reason to define present existence which is leading things into a fixed outcome to move, project, and catapult, the universal permeating substance that defines everything, forward to the next predetermination date which perhaps is just a split second from now.

LJ's deep analytical mind pondered this type of anti-solipsistic esoteric cosmology, created from openly embracing the monads of enlightenment he found on the etheric plane he discovered through the profoundly deep alpha wave meditation induced by experimenting with the various spiritual awareness Upps of envisionment and creative cognition, which appear to tap into the astral plane of information, or more simply the Akashic records. One finds themselves asking oneself, "what knowledge are you seeking?" "What Varna do you wish to obtain?" It is like receiving information in your dreams and waking up to remembering it and finding it may be useful. Once tapped into the Akashic hall of records one feels surrounded by it and enveloped inside its infinite enlightenment, euphoric with wisdom, knowledge, understanding, and creativity. The residual affinity leaves a feeling like being a single helium particle in an immeasurable Mylar balloon. You are individually aware but engulfed as part of the oneness of the whole keeping things timelessly aloft.

Although not much of a drinker, or any other type of abuser, Matt found out during his annual autumn check-up that his liver was in a state of severe deterioration and in need of immediate engagement. He worried; was *his* number now coming up while just still in his forties? After cross checking current inventories his physician ordered him to travel to Nevada's National Jelly Fish Organ Facility for Regenerative Medicine that same day to begin the process of being individually tailored with a genetic replacement. The Center got its name from the salt water nuisance which came to unlock the secrets of lab grown transplant organs raised in bio-tanks from personally extracted primordial staple cells.

In addition to the organ growing lab the huge complex also housed an enormous organ donor bank stockpiled with a countless supply of statically preserved standard replacement organs to go along with featuring their state of the art cytocompatibility bio-printing lab. Once Matt's new liver was cultivated a three dimensional practice model was burned for a preliminary rehearsal surgery, which predictably went off without a hitch. The whole replacement process took around ten weeks before he could begin the healing and adaptation phase. During this time he had to endure some traditional therapies at the Treatment Center adjacent from the growing lab. On the bright side, throughout this stage of the difficult ordeal, he was also able to get a slightly congested somewhat failing aortic heart valve replaced. A new valve exhibiting mechanical heterogeneity was generated by the 3D cytocompatibility bio-printing lab, after metallic physical vapor deposition through a piezo-actuator controlled stencil mask prepped the valve. When Matt was finished being monitored for an additional month in one of the outer wings of the vast facility, he was finally medically cleared and permitted to return home.

The spring rolled back around in a blink of an eye that medically burdened winter. It was nice to experience a milder winter that year following the previous two year's harsh colonial winters. Spring generally appeared to emerge earlier and earlier. Many areas with their mild winters seemed to experience only three seasons. Summer will cool off quickly changing over to winter skipping right through the short lived temperate fall season. Six or Seven months of summer and a good four of winter and whatever is left you can call it what you will. The winter's gloomy drear drags on for a good four months and then spring heats right back into summer, before you know it, lasting right back into another winter once again.

Matt began seeing what seemed to be the insignificance of his own small role and miniscule place, which he felt silently left a near invisible footprint. Attach this with his widened view of the expansive Mother Earth, which suddenly appeared to be a much larger place materialized in the mind of this fortunate and grateful survivor, his indebted and more appreciative soul now reflected ever more on the vastness of our global surroundings. He calculated, if the number of square miles on the surface of the Planet is roughly 200 million and we could, just two dimensionally, theoretically fit 625,000 individuals shoulder to shoulder on one square mile, well it is easy for one to do the math and see that a person alone isn't so big, just a speck of pepper on a city block.

He also contemplated how Implant Phone evolution and its implications, not unlike the addictions of internet and cell phones, made for a hectic life, even though it would be ever more instantaneous, portable, and useful. Ironically on the go communication technology started off quite large like a phone flipping to the size of a dress shoe. Then they were desired ever smaller and smaller till they were nearly inoperable by human fingertips, and then only to come full circle where their convenient display screens were preferred ever larger once again. Think of where we have come since the suitcase sized battlefield phones and radios that GIs once had to tote around, or the size of a break dancer's D battery powered boom box radio in the 1980's. As these are just modern day recent examples, it has been going on all throughout history, being anything from a pocket knife to an animal skin water flask. Humans have always desired to have their technology at their side either for necessity, convenience, or pleasure. Of course all of these conveniences make the world appear smaller and smaller as if Antarctica and Italy are either next door or just a hop skip and a click apart from each other. Then, now, comes the Implant Phone. Huge in power, small in inconvenience. Connected directly, one is not even able to become aware that it is there as a part of themselves; and transmission of verbal communication fumbles out as a lost art. Although technology communicates instant data, which shrinks down human separation and makes the world seem smaller and smaller, there is the easily forgotten fact that our planet is still quite enormously large and your exact location upon it is always in reality going to be only a microscopic point.

About the same time that the maiden mining expeditions harvesting the space rock Vesta were first landing the preparatory equipment required to strip and retrieve the coveted precious metals and solar elements silently awaiting to be shipped back home to Earth, LJ and Asher were deciding on the exact date and time they wanted designated to perform the commencement of their Spousal Union of Domestic Equality, as legalized by the PRA, or Partnership Rights Act, quite a few years beforehand. For one thing the two needed to reserve their slot at Peace Church, but also, besides, maybe, the date when one first met their significant other, the anniversary is the most important day of the year for a couple desiring to commit to share the rest of their lives together. This is because as this significant and noteworthy day comes to be each year, it is celebrated and observed as a milestone marking the fidelity and evaluating the good, bad, or in between moments and events which have took place and been shared throughout another year together. The wedding anniversary symbolizes being able to look back and reflect on the traversing of another year's joyful encounters and shared struggles which anchor partners together, till there is a bundle of decades to look back on with pride, contentment, and peace, knowing you are spending a lifetime with your true love. This of course if you actually are with your genuine soulmate, such as was the unmistakable case with the highly devoted pair of Asher and LJ who never engaged in any type of promiscuous degenerate morality acts such as cheating, swinging, or a threescumski.

It was an exciting time for the whole Notts family throughout the course of this momentous event. LJ and Asher were paired up like a match made in heaven, destined from a very young age to be true companions enduring endlessly forever. The two clicked and complimented each other like identical twins, finishing each other's sentences with their likeminded thinking. Connected by more than just a wired link through an Implant Phone, their human magnetism flowed continuous into the odic breath of their argon thule. Their ceaseless enthalpy, the everlasting divine spark. That which is illuminating translucent. The perpetual pulsating ambient sparkle between the two kindred spirits forever linked together, two becoming one. Two separate individuals becoming one eternal soul.

It wasn't long before the two men considered the different options of completing their hatchling family, such as adoption, which was what LJ's parents Matt and Amber were briefly deliberating now that their only child and his spouse were no longer going to be physically living in the main house of the family estate, only residing there as nothing more than a telepresence. Asher and LJ could advertise for a surrogate to complete the task the old fashioned way or through artificial insemination. Either way they may still need a womb. They could choose any egg donor, yet nonetheless the child would not be a true part of each of them as they desired. Who would it be to give the DNA? A crap shoot produced from the solicitation of wild nocturnal encounters with a surrogate? Twinning one from each was a possibility, but then again the newborn child isn't wholly a splice of each of them. The science of the day made it easily possible to create the child they conceived in their hearts, however controversial it may have been to the few close minded and frightened fundamentalist still lurking around afraid of the acceptance of change. Some people are leaders and some people are followers. It is up to the individual to decide to ripple the waves and effect the status quo.

Asher had the 21st century perfectionism down to a T. His mother-in-law Amanda provided the perfect smile which could win the admiration of any heart. Through looking into another's eyes, which are the window to the soul, with his corrected large flushing deep blue irises ever pulsating radiantly in a face to face encounter, one would become mesmerized. His proper posture was tuned to be straight as an arrow. The adjusted set thickness of his wavy hair screamed movie star. His naturally supplemented athletic build provided ease of mobility through all urban jungles as well as any sparsely inhabited wilderness terrain he might explore. It seemed any man versus nature challenge would be conquered with ease by his, biologically unassuming, fluid athletic movements. He could climb mountains and dive the depths. Asher pretty much could have been with any companion he so desired. A rewritten flawless creation, the revised Asher dedicated his tweaked life only to LJ, and then later to their impeccably engineered biological twins.

The Clinton Genetic Research Center was the full service facility the two men would need to visit. Subterranean advancements propulsioned cutting edge medicine and science beneath the scrutiny of hardline factions woefully fearful of inevitable change. Small mindedness doesn't see that the altering of the status quo is what is continually cycling around the planet minute by minute to advance time forward, proceeding unstoppably into the future. Evolution is an alteration of the fixed, and a natural course of nature. Change should be embraced and not attempted to be prevented by those wishing only to hinder the progression of the natural modification and advancement unfolding toward a collision course with the singularity of humanity and nature, the environment, and Mother Earth. The seeds of time germinate in the womb of evolution which is knotted to the navel of the maturing mother Earth, making a status quo impossible as it becomes a flowing fluid concept perpetuating life forward in its relentless journey through time.

Imagine the passing on of information from one person to another by word of mouth. After going through hundreds of embellished explanations the original details, passed along by the first person to relay the message, is in all likely hood going to be skewed, if even only slightly, by the time it gets to the current custodian of the communication and its interpretation. Now take the passing on of genes and the diversity of the millions of individuals pooling the material to the next generation. The same as in all of nature, little adjustments and tweaks pass along to each new life created from the distributing of biological information from the previous inhabitants.

All new things until they are known and understood likely will be scrutinized and feared before they are accepted. People once scouringly scorned, "horses could in no way be replaced by the horseless carriage." "A firearm won't ever be able to replace the potency of a sword." "A home phone land line will always be a necessity because mobile phones are just a fad and aren't for everyone." It goes on and on. Who would actually pay for water? Isn't it free like radio? "That is absurd." But put it into a processed tasting plastic bottle and a new chapter has begun. New technology simply can sometimes be hard to understand at first. It isn't truly believed until it is received and acclimated into society. When first suggested it was hard to fathom that cars could be driven without human control, and now it is hard to comprehend being in one that isn't self-piloted. It is all about a gradual ever changing perception of who we are and what we can become.

If LJ and Asher had any arguments in their marriage about growing a family, it was certain that the precisely fashioned Asher, who at this age of his life had a belief that advancements would keep him alive and young for hundreds of years, had no scruples with using cutting edge science to achieve their genetic goals for a perfect child. To create, that which would be considered in Asher and LJ's mind, a flawless human being, that in which the Genesis Wing of the Clinton Genetic Research Center helped produce by combing the amino acids and proteins of the two married men together, and later transferring the two growing engineered embryos into the surrogate womb. Two healthy boys to be birthed from the combined DNA of the two matrimonially joined men. Down the line, as their imprint manipulation children grew into adulthood, LJ and Asher would kiddingly joke how the boys were the splice of their life.

Imprint Manipulation allowed responsible family persons with the financial means to procreate their own biological child. Those who were interested in the ethical opposition had no power to stop the advancement, had to wake up and proceed to the future, and had to realize and accept the fact that it was not worth fighting against if it was that important for a burdened couple to go to such great lengths as somatic splicing of a clone, egg nuclear transfer, and creating an egg from primordial germ cells for the purpose of having stem cell DNA enucleated inside of it to allow the mixing up of the two individual's DNA, which in reality was no less effective than the conventional mix up process that has been occurring from sexual relations over the millennia. Some people would like to argue against anything new, changing the status quo, or simply controversial. But it is hard to argue against nature when there surely are intelligent species out there that don't need two individuals to continue on with the success of their genetic race. It happens right here on Mother Earth with certain aquatic and land species as well as on an undiscovered massive scale of microscopic organisms. Surely the path that LJ and Asher chose to give family care and love to a child is just as good if not better than the life a rape child left upon the doorstep of a firehouse might have to endure. For loving couples unable to conceive it was comforting to have a fresh alternative for family formation. There was even the case where one fortyish couple used the man's primordial germ cells to create the egg and the woman's to create the sperm for their healthy well cared for child.

The imprint manipulation children Adam and Ahmo would become the next generation of the Notts line. The two siblings would be destined to together continue the family fortunes onward into the next age. Adam would receive Asher's sir name of Lake, and Ahmo would go under Notts. Their childhood was nothing less than normal for the time. If anything they were excelling above the norm and were living unassumingly in an upper echelon. Fortunately, while the twins were growing up, they were in no way discriminated upon, and most likely wouldn't have been even if there was a breach in the privacy of their situation, as could often be the case for young children being reared in a unique environment going against the "norm."

The two young men grew up to clear away their own separate paths while still maintaining a close impenetrable bond between one another. Ahmo, more quiet and reserved, seemed to forever be drawn to the university and believed a person's commitment to schooling was an obligation that might never be finished. An intellectual following after his father LJ (more than his father Asher), Ahmo spent a career as a professor of ethical studies. The two likeminded existential thinkers, Ahmo and LJ, would have long conversations going back and forth on the history and implications of society's development. Ahmo felt a need to give to the progression of humanity through nurturing an individual's use, understanding, and empowerment of education. Many of his students and under studies took his enthusiasm for knowledge to heart, followed in his footsteps, and went on to achieve great humanitarian achievements through their academically positive promotions, and the contagious Notts, undying pay it forward attitude.

On the other hand the other half of the twins, Adam, took more after their father Asher. Adam was outgoing and desired to be hands on, in touch with nature, and rather than give back solely intellectually with his mind, he made his career, donating back to the spirit known as Mother Earth, all of the numerous resources he had at his disposal, notwithstanding his motivational powers of persuasion by example and his energetic, physical, go-getter attitude. An iconic humanitarian his legacy was defined in his tireless contributions in launching the Coral Reef Oceanic Habitat Sanctuary (CROHS). A project in which he applied his eternal love for nature and the ocean, while utilizing Notts monetary assets and connections. Even though he was a Midwest boy, Adam was drawn to the ocean through an inherited unexplainable attraction akin to our primal DNA, which fosters roots still buried alive inside all humans to this day, beginning from an awakening point sometime after first creation.

The oceanic haven was created by a worldwide alliance of nations to preserve marine habitat for future generations. A staunch proponent from the beginning, Adam propelled the project forward, and later sat on the board overseeing its operations for over twenty years. The building of a man made coral reef was nothing new for the ocean to see. A clump of old concrete situated in the right location would draw marine life around it to build a natural habit simply nudged forward by the initiativeness of doing something. Coral Reefs, the rainforests of the sea, had been moved away from human sprawl in the past. It was simply a matter of agreeing upon the necessity and proper location for the marine sanctuary, and then implementing the immense project. The countries of South America, which saw human progress and sprawl create a massive reduction to their ecologically significant rain forest coverage aiding the planet, acceptingly entertained the idea of allowing this marine sanctuary off of one its shores. Of course this enormous undertaking, which would one day become the largest coral reef chain on the planet, would take up a huge part of the ocean, be strictly regulated, and could not be readily economically harvested. This was because creating the massive coral reef habitat would only be a small part of the Marine Sanctuary.

With the Andes Mountains naturally cutting off mass inhabitants of South America, the unprecedented large scale westward migration did not occur until after the CROHS Project had been long established. The relatively sparsely populated coast of Chile became the least demanding economic evil effecting fishing related communities, even though with the return humanitarian aid offered, and later received by the fortunate philanthropic country, many countries around the globe were willing to have their outlying International waters designated as the conservancy zone dedicated to the preservation of Mother Earth's marine life. Whales born in captivity where released here to begin a natural migratory path which would become home based out of this new human created, terraformed setting, located in the South Pacific. Really not that far from the Palau Island Chain, corals from this ancient habitat were used to help seed and establish the roots for what would become one of the greatest new age "natural" wonders of man's engineering prowess. Here, and in other parts of nature, it wasn't uncommon, and was accepted, for certain species to have only one sex, one individual unit, procreate itself. The evolution of Natural selection, a branch breeding out flaws and disease from within itself.

The greatest modern day wonders would spring up from the dry sands across the globe. The sparse dessert landscapes of America for instance, were a raw and open blank canvas awaiting industrial sprawl to rise up, transform, and exploit the vast physical geography of the inherently undeveloped and uncluttered native environment situated in the center of the western half of the U.S. This receptive chunk of Earth offered an ideal dry and stable climate to locate the next generation of new age, sustainable, clean, hygienic power facilities (HPF), that would produce and supply the electricity to accommodate the growing needs of an ever multiplying census count. Reminisceful of FDR Public Works Administration, National Industrial Recovery Act, New Deal-like public works projects from long ago, the construction of these hygienic energy production facilities was only part of the planned development plotted out for this expendable track of real estate.

A state, or perhaps even country, unto itself all clustered into one vast region, this greatest of all manmade wonders, New Desert, was a threefold energy production endeavor on a massive scope unmatched in the history of mankind. Some would argue it to be greater than all other energy endeavors put together due to its colossal magnitude. Designed to sustain the western United States and parts of Canada and Mexico for centuries to come, wind, solar and water assisted power generation would produce the needed hygienic energy required for this bold and taunting terraformation, as well as the future needs of the entire western half of the continent, as the next great human migration rushed to populate the booming region on a near unfathomable unprecedented scale.

Sure people need energy and a city to live in, but more than anything else, to survive, there is also a need for water. To think of how there is a lack of water, as it is rising up and changing the map around us while swallowing up frontage on the face of the ever changing and continuously evolving Mother Earth, seems inherently absurd. After how many thousands of years of human existence and continual advancement alongside a fundamental need for water, while a majority of the sustaining Mother Earth's surface is engulfed by the most precious of liquids derived from the most abundant and basic of elements, clean drinking water reserves should be at the forefront of a society's technological advancement at any and all costs. It is like not getting a needed heart surgery because of the expense and just letting yourself die out, which seemed to be the course and fate that millions of thirsty citizens were headed towards.

A series of canals, aided with natural canyon formations, were dug to divert and stem the rising ocean water of the Pacific down into the new Southwest. Channeling and filtering salt water down into the repurposed dessert region of America with a second and third, more advanced and productive, Hoover damn-type electricity production facility along the way to the final destination, the new Great Lake, Lake Delano, containing a thousand year supply of fresh drinking water. As the water flowed down the desalination process into its final destination, the salt would gradually filter out into rock walls and special filtration screens at the top of locks pinching the water downstream. A Dead Sea type lake was located at the head of the first stage of filtration. Hybrid vegetations, combining leafy vegetables and tubers with marine flora and plant life, were created in the lab so that food sources could be grown and irrigated along the few scattered parts of this salty shore that were *not* destined for resort villages and economically lucrative tourism settings.

Advanced solar collection fields sprinkled the once arid dessert floor across a large flat and open expanse. At first there was only a small beginning phase constructed able to meet the power needs for roughly one million people, but enough area was set aside to increase the facility one hundred fold with much of the future plans involving the solar fields rising up rather than sprawling out and gobbling up soon to be limited and very valuable real estate. As Photovoltaic solar improvements sleekly sailed ahead they mimicked and pirated nature's cold blooded reptile charging-up abilities as well as the bee's perfected honeycomb storage capacities. Inconspicuously solar collection technology quickly advanced positively throughout the 21st century as it adapted itself silently, nearly invisible to a preoccupied expectful culture. Cutting edge closed loop manufacturing processes would contain and recycle 99.9% off the fabrication materials as multi-junction solar cells simultaneously reached 95% photoelectric efficiency effect through methods involving heating deuterium enriched heavy water to run the Stirling engines producing the renewable hygienic energy. There is no doubt when something works it can go into full scale production in a relatively short time after the first successful tests are ran off. A good example is the 20th century historical fact that the Hiroshima bomb was dropped only three weeks after the triumphant tests were detonated out in these same dry dessert sands.

Wind farms tethered up into the Jetstream by their diamond clad nano crystalline thread capped off the jewel city of Democritus which was a prosperous industrial section atop mountainess high ground. These wind farms were situated part way up a larger structure reaching far up above the Earth's surface. An elevator to a launching platform free of surface gravity and offering rotational assist was set up above the hygienic wind facility which powered this vast section of New Desert by the continuous source of wind energy powered by the Earth's rotation. Dug out to step into the valley, the sheltered East side provided many of the construction resources needed for New Desert. Vast agriculture and residential areas were tiered into the terrain stepping to the east, but also pyramiding to the north and south of center where a passage way was created to link the west coast. A series of several high speed transport trains allowed commuters to make the trip between the West coast and "The Pass" in, bank tube suction like, relatively short time. Also referred to as the Gateway, the term The Pass was reverbing old west terminology for the new western U.S. of New Desert. Two large signs promoting philosophical expression and enlightenment greeted travelers coming through the pass. One declared that, "One Needs to Pass through For Another to Move Forward." The other read coming out of one of the tunnel accelerators: "And He said Let there Be Light. And through the silence their Eyes were Opened".

Like many man made engineering wonders the economic value of the awe inspiring novelty was considerably incorporated into the planning and construction to provide future sources of revenue and income while promoting world-wide attraction as thee place to go to and see in the course of your lifetime. The immense theme parks and mountainside cable rides coupled with the complete interactive telepresence would have been hard for early 21st century minds to grasp and first understand if leaped right into these modern cities without the gradual adaptation required for the understanding and manipulation of all new technology and cutting edge advancements. New Desert was seemingly an endless chain of engineering marvels situated in a concise central region transformed and cut out of what was basically raw wasteland. The whole set up of tourist attractions and destinations was designed to either keep you and your money there or coming back again and again to receive more unbridled stimulation of the senses.

In their lifetimes the twins, Ahmo and Adam, saw many amazing and exciting advancements came along to encompass mankind, and in their own right grew into respected individuals that any family would be proud to call their own. Their parents LJ and Asher quietly went on their way content with the two boys they had produced and guided into adulthood. Matt and Amber lived well into the 21st century with Matt outlasting his beloved wife by nearly twenty years. Of course, eventually, Matt too would pass. Medical Science can only keep the human body going for so long before something greater steps in and decides that it is time to move forward. At this point there is no choice but to throw in the towel. With Amber already passed, and he living in a tired rickety body, Matt would leave it up to the future generations of his line to decide how long they wanted to delay the inevitable and perhaps buy into a cyber-generated replacement body that would be either the abnormally muscular robotic looking one, being more synthesized over machine, or the child like lab grown replacement body that resembled a feeble Extra Terrestrial alien gray type, with the advantages of full human perception, touch, and emotion.

As his luminous golden years waned and came to be clarified, and after most of the dynamic events of his radiant enlightened lifetime had come to pass, the prophetic LJ dissected in his mind's vocabulary the difference between human kind and humanity. To him human kind made him think of us, homo-sapiens, you and I as human beings, a physical genetic race of mortal beings struggling to stave off extinction. On the other hand humanity was something more to him, something bigger. Humanity surpasses a simple living and breathing creature. It is an essence of all breathing creatures living with an instinctive perception of right and wrong going beyond the first and final heart thump. Not mortal but evolving to a higher awareness and fullness, fulfilling the destiny of thousands of years of struggles, bloodshed, advancements and enlightenment. He liked to think that even if the human race became extinct humanity would still live on, on the Earth continuously, through the eternal order of nature.

This made him wonder about a higher power and the commonality of the sense of an all-seeing eye which outshines, encircles, eclipses, and rises above the individual mortality towards a greater good overseeing the transcendence of a humbled humanity towards the fundamental linear goals encompassed within the order of the cyclic infinite number of the universe awaiting the perpetual chaos of creation to settle back into its orderly patterns. In the end, after being worn down from years of intellectual contemplation, LJ's final conclusions were that all questions and answers about the meaning of life and existence were to forever be ambiguous, shaded, and uncertain even beyond the short complex physical life destined to die out.

A human transcendence of collectiveness had occurred through the spiritual awakening via the acceptance and use of collective recognition awareness Upps which uncaged the minds of the masses to bring together the spirit of all souls existing unbounded by the limitations of time, breathe, and dimension. Every breathing human being is walking a fine line between the worlds, where the physical world is the only plane where a body is temporarily needed, and once the time came where we were able to readily, easily, and coherently access our non physical spirit out of body, there is a realm in which our inner fire is only a short step away from igniting outward to join the others which have come beforehand, and after, who are together shining outwardly eternal, linked to all as one great glow. Through this evolution and awakening of human spirit the twins Adam and Ahmo could spiritually know the strength of Grandpa Notts, the flamboyant character of Uncle Henry, the short lived yet beautiful force of Aunt Amanda, as well the atmosphere of all huddled together as one essence. Ours became an Earth where the past walked with the present and the future. The awaiting spirit of humanity one with the universe.

Of course the Notts story continues on proceeding in time, but it is generally the same story. Not wholly that much different than the daily struggles and exhalations flowing forth from the beginning of our book or from within the lives of Grandpa Notts and Uncle Henry. The life and death interactions cycle onward, not starting over but continuing forward from the past to repeat the same human emotions and curiosities burning up inside the never ending soul struggling for answers from within. The characters, environment, and situations change some, as the clock ticks forward, a brief breath snapping one in and out of a momentary reality, a hick-up in nature's course. A lifetime which is nothing more than a single instantaneous second ticked off a millennium of actions and insights. Insignificant overall but most important, valuable, and precious in this so treasured of realities coveted during one's own momentary stay.

Wake up and smell the coffee. Proceed to the future. The two matrimonially joined men, LJ and Asher, sold Grandpa Notts' relinquished Japanese Samurai swords for hundreds of millions. This after cashing almost all of the families other assets, and started a clinic to provide a Mother Earth with a female free existence. Oh the male chauvinist supremacist would love to hear such that, but maybe it all ends up the other way around. Free and liberated Females unite and rise up to Splice their future released and unburdened of male rule and chocked full of liberal value. All the same. The outcome is pretty much the same in all speculative scenarios. Borderline on the fence issues which contain right and wrong, where both sides are right and both sides are wrong, where acceptance and coexistence with the solutions are the ambiguity.